Praise for *A Cup of Tea*

"With deceptive simplicity and appealingly uncluttered prose, Ephron weaves a morality tale that moves inexorably from mannered start to jarring finish."
—*People*

"A jewel. . . . This novel will plunge you into New York City in the turbulent year of 1917 and will keep you enthralled. . . . A page-turner from start to finish, Ms. Ephron's spare novel has classic proportions."
—*West Coast Review of Books*

"A fine book." —*Los Angeles Times*

"Compelling in its tightness but never lacking proper development, this is a sterling novel." —*Booklist*

"Ephron excels in re-creating the aura of an era. . . . [A] careful evocation of the period."
—*Atlanta Journal-Constitution*

"A graceful writer with a good eye for period detail."
Star

"Ephron tells this ⋯⋯⋯⋯⋯⋯⋯⋯⋯ tly, with an old-fashi⋯⋯⋯⋯⋯⋯⋯⋯ in its time frame." ⋯⋯ *ton Star*

"This book most assuredly will be any woman's cup of tea." —*Oklahoma City Oklahoman*

"All of the period detail is correct right down to the last streetlamp. . . . Ephron gives us a rich situation and a carefully drawn setting." —*Publishers Weekly*

"A little trinket of a story . . . with pretty period details and an appealing spareness to her prose." —*Baltimore Sun*

"Ephron weaves a solid tale of love and betrayal." —*Hartford Courant*

"This book is smooth and seamlessly written with a screenwriter's sure hand for manipulation in short spaces." —*Los Angeles Times*

Herman Agopian

About the Author

AMY EPHRON is a novelist and screenwriter. She is the author of *One Sunday Morning*, *White Rose: Una Rosa Blanca*, *Cool Shades*, *Bruised Fruit*, and *Biodegradable Soap*, and lives with her family in Los Angeles.

Also by Amy Ephron

One Sunday Morning

White Rose: Una Rosa Blanca

Biodegradable Soap

Bruised Fruit

Cool Shades

A
Cup of Tea

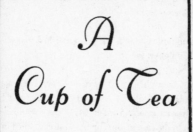

A Cup of Tea

A Novel of 1917

Amy Ephron

HARPER PERENNIAL

HARPER ● PERENNIAL

First Harper Perennial edition published 2005.

Library of Congress Cataloging-in-Publication Data
Ephron, Amy.
    A cup of tea : a novel of 1917 / Amy Ephron.
        p. cm.
    ISBN-10: 0-06-078620-5
    ISBN-13: 978-0-06-078620-5
    1. Upper class women—Fiction. 2. New York (N.Y.)—Fiction. I. Title.

PS3555.P47C86 2005
813'.54—dc22

2004063520

05 06 07 08 09 PENN/RRDH 10 9 8 7 6 5 4 3 2 1

For
Nora, Delia, and Hallie

A
Cup of Tea

A young woman stood under a street lamp. It was difficult to make her out at first because she was standing almost in shadow and the mist from the ground, the rain, and approaching night made the air and the street seem similarly gray and damp. It was dusk. A light rain was falling.

A man walked up and solicited her. It startled her. She shook her head and turned away. Without another thought of her, he hailed a cab which stopped for him at once. She pulled the thin sweater, hardly protection from the rain, tighter around her shoulders as she stepped back from the curb to avoid the spray of dirt and water as the taxi pulled away.

*D*own the street, a very different scene. In an antique store famous for accepting only quality estates and European shipments where not a speck of dust had ever been allowed to gather on the shelves, a woman, slightly older than the woman under the street lamp, stood in front of a display case. Her name was Rosemary Fell. Her clothing was exquisite. Her dark hair framed her face even though in the morning she had put it up severely but it was of such thickness that no amount of coaxing, particularly in damp weather, could ever get it not to fall, a few moments later, softly around her face. She liked the effect and would sometimes play with one of the curls about her forehead when she wanted to appear as though she was thinking of something. Her stance was casual, almost disinterested, her gloves and coat still on as though she had not yet decided whether she had stopped in long enough to actually consider anything. Mr. Rhenquist, the owner of the antique store, was all over her.

"You see, I love my things," he said, in low respectful tones, waiting for her reaction. "I would rather not part with them than sell them to someone who has not that"—he gestured with his hand displaying a pale green jade ring on his ring finger that Rosemary could not help but notice—"feeling of appreciation which is so rare."

He unrolled a tiny square of blue velvet and pressed it on the glass counter with his pale finger-tips. It was an enamel box he had been keeping for her with a glaze so fine it looked as though it had been baked in cream. "I saved this for you."

On its lid, a minute creature stood under a flowery tree. A hat, no bigger than a geranium petal, with green ribbons, hung from a branch. And a pink cloud like a watchful cherub floated above the creature's head. Rosemary took her hands out of her long gloves to examine the box.

She set the box down as though she had no interest other than to look at it. She said, after a moment, "It's beautiful." And then very casually asked, "How much?"

For a moment, Mr. Rhenquist seemed not to hear her, or else he was considering the price. "For you . . ." He leaned in and whispered to her as if it would be impolite to speak of this out loud.

She made a face and then looked vague. She stared at an etched glass figurine on a shelf directly above his head. She reached for her gloves and started to put them on. And then, as she was about to leave, she said, "I guess I have no choice," as her eye was caught by something else in the display case.

Rhenquist saw what she was looking at and without a word, took it carefully out of the case and put it on the glass for her to see. It was a letter opener, simple yet ornate, silver slightly etched in gold. She took it in her hand to gauge its weight. Its blade was thin and razor sharp. For a moment, it caught the light from the overhead lamp and glinted slightly.

"I'll take it, too," said Rosemary laughing. "At least it will be something useful."

"Of course, Miss Fell," said Rhenquist as he put the porcelain box carefully in a velvet bag. With a pen carved out of mother-of-pearl, he discreetly scribbled a number on a piece of paper and turned it toward her.

It was fairly extravagant. She could sometimes be

such a wasteful thing. But what good was it to have money if one didn't sometime indulge.

Rosemary nodded and reached into her purse for her chequebook. She wrote him a cheque, ripped it from her chequebook, and casually left it on the counter.

Rosemary watched as Rhenquist wrapped the velvet bag and letter opener deftly in brown paper, his pale hands amazing for their dexterity. Nothing rare was ever broken here.

He handed her the parcel and bowed his head slightly. It was clear he would have kept them for her forever. Rosemary smiled and started to leave. As she opened the door, the bells on the shop door jingled slightly.

It was still raining but Rosemary didn't seem to mind as she walked down the street to the flower shop. Smoke was rising from the potholes contributing to the mist and griminess of the city.

On the corner, there was still the shape of the woman standing under the streetlight. It was more than an accident of birth and a length of pavement that separated these two women.

The salesgirl followed Rosemary as she made her way through the crowded florist shop a few doors down from the antique store. "I'll have those and those." Rosemary pointed to some lilies and irises. "Four bunches of those. And I'll take those sweet pink roses."

The salesgirl held some lilacs up for her to see.

"No, no lilacs." So this next didn't come out too harshly, Rosemary smiled. "I hate lilacs. They have no shape. And that smell, you know they're there before you even walk into the room." She laughed. "But give me those stumpy little tulips, the red and white ones." In her mind she was figuring that they would sit prettily in the gray stone vase in her bedroom while the longer stemmed lilies could be arranged downstairs in the dining room in the pewter vase.

Her thoughts drifted to how she might get out of Florence Pemberton's invitation to lunch the following day. Flo was always so serious. Flo's life was so uneventful. Rosemary would have cut her years ago if it hadn't been for the fact that Florence Pemberton was Philip Alsop's cousin and Rosemary had known since she was a little girl that she was going to marry Philip Alsop. But now that the wedding was six months off, couldn't she afford to be a little less attentive to Florence Pemberton or did it require that she be more so?

She seemed distracted as the salesgirl trimmed her flowers and wrapped them in paper. She took some money out of her wallet to pay. And then the salesgirl walked in front of her out of the shop to the car, carrying the immense white paper armful.

Rosemary stopped on the pavement. Her eye was caught by the creature with enormous eyes holding her sweater around her with reddened hands. It was raining harder now and with it came the darkness spinning down like ashes. Rosemary walked over to her. "Are you all right?"

The woman nodded. She looked at Rosemary and

hesitated before speaking. "C-could I——?" the creature stammered. "Could I ask you for some money—enough for a cup of tea?"

Rosemary couldn't help but notice it wasn't the voice of a street-person. "Have you *no* money?" she asked.

"None at all, ma'am," was the answer.

Rosemary considered this a moment. She looked over at her car and her driver who stood waiting for her. The rain was coming down in sheets around them.

It *was* like something one would read about, to find a girl in the dusk and bring her home for tea. Ought she to have been frightened that the girl would turn out to be a thief or half-mad. She didn't look half-mad. She looked like someone who life had done a wrong turn to, who had never had the proper opportunity. And think how she would feel if she could successfully show this poor creature that life could be wonderful, that all women were sisters, that the world was full of possibilities. She would help her get on her feet. It was an act of altruism. What good was it to have power, if one couldn't be beneficent some of the time.

She could hear herself saying to her friends, "It just seemed like such an adventure," as she turned and said, "Why don't you come home to tea with me?"

The woman stepped back from her.

"Why don't you?" said Rosemary. "Come home with me now in my car and have tea. At least until it stops raining."

The woman protested. "I couldn't," she said. "It wouldn't be—"

Rosemary interrupted her. "—right?! Why not?!" She put her hand on the woman's arm and started to propel her towards the car.

Rosemary's driver had opened the car door and was holding an umbrella over their heads.

"Don't be frightened," said Rosemary with the sort of confidence you have when you've never had to be frightened of anything. "Why shouldn't you come home with me?"

The inside of the car was leather. There was a pale brown cashmere afghan folded neatly on the seat, a small nosegay of flowers in a bud vase attached to the seatback that separated the rear of the car from the driver. The engine had been idling and the inside of the car was warm. The girl managed a small smile as Rosemary hurdled her into the warmth and safety of the backseat of the car.

And, for a moment, in the backseat, Eleanor, for that is the name she would tell you if asked, Eleanor Smith, had a moment to be nervous.

Did the driver look at her disapprovingly ... of course, he did, but it wouldn't be his place to speak about it. He did seem to take a long time though to shut the car door and walk around to the front, close the umbrella, get in, finally, and shift the car into gear. Long enough for her to worry that this could end (as it must certainly end) before it had even started.

"*O*h Gertrude, don't look like that . . ." thought Rosemary as she saw the expression on her housekeeper's face when she appeared at the door to help with the packages. "Not that anything I do should surprise her by now! . . ."

"We don't need help, Gertrude, thanks," said Rosemary. "Just tea . . . and sandwiches." And she hurried the poor girl out of sight up the stairs to spare her being stared at. And then shouted down to Gertrude again, "Not just butter. Make some with chicken, would you? We'll have it up in my room."

Halfway up the stairs, Rosemary stopped and took

her gloves off. She took a deep breath. "It's just too cold out. I'm frozen through. I can imagine how you must feel!" She put her arm lightly on the young woman's back. "We'll go up to my room. It's cozy there."

Gertrude stayed where she was at the bottom of the stairs and looked after them distrustfully. Rosemary turned and saw her and laughed. "We don't need help, Gertrude, honest. Just tea."

Gertrude walked off to the pantry grumbling, as if she didn't have enough to do besides make an unscheduled meal . . . and what was Rosemary up to, anyway?

But ever since Rosemary's mother died, going on nine years ago, Gertrude had been the mother-hen variety of housekeeper, peckish and overbearing but in a completely endearing way. Maybe she was always that way but when Mrs. Fell was alive there was a direct chain of command and order in the household and ever since she'd passed, it had sort of been betwixt and between with Gertrude not knowing whether it was Rosemary, the woman of the house, giving her orders or Rosemary, the child, whom she was obliged to be telling what to do. Not that she'd ever been able to stop Rosemary from doing anything.

There was a fire burning in the fireplace in Rosemary's room, a funny assortment of flowers that looked as if it had been thrown together from a garden in a vase on the table in front of the couch. Rosemary threw her coat and hat off carelessly onto the back of a velvet chair. The young woman stood not far from the fire, holding her sweater around her. She seemed unsure of what she was to do, if it were all right for her to warm herself by the fire or take a seat.

"You are soaked through," said Rosemary in the way a big sister would to a little girl and then because she knew it would take some prodding, she helped the girl off with her sweater and hung it over the screen of the fireplace to dry. "There."

The young woman stood holding onto the back of the sofa as though it was all that stood between her and the floor as Rosemary reached distractedly for a cigarette on the mantel.

And then the creature spoke. "I'm sorry, I think I may—" She braced herself and tried to gain control again. "I've never fainted."

Rosemary put the cigarette down. "Oh, how thoughtless of me." She opened the door and called down the stairs. "Could you hurry those sandwiches, Gertrude?"

Rosemary raced about and took a decanter off the table. She poured a glass of brandy which she offered to the woman.

And then the creature spoke again. "I don't—I don't drink brandy."

Rosemary smiled. "It will revive you. At least, I think it will revive you. Would you feel better if I had one . . . ?" She poured herself a brandy and took a sip. "Here, now we've both gone off."

She held the glass out again to the woman, and this time it was accepted and downed, rather quickly, although Rosemary didn't notice as there was a knock on the door at exactly this moment.

"Oh, the tea. That will help. You just sit there."

Rosemary watched as the woman collapsed into the softness of the sofa.

She opened the door to a rather sour-faced Gertrude holding a tray. "I'll take it, Gertrude, thanks." She closed the door before Gertrude could quite get a look inside and set the tray down on the table. "There."

The woman helped herself to a tea sandwich and ravenously took a bite.

"They're good, aren't they?" said Rosemary trying to be polite. Rosemary delicately bit into a cucumber sandwich as the woman finished hers. "Have as many as you want, please." And then because she wanted to make conversation, make it seem as though it were an ordinary afternoon for this poor creature, she went on much as she would to anyone she was trying to make conversation with. "I should learn to cook but with Gertrude here . . ." She gestured with her hand sort of vaguely and then trailed off. "Do you cook?"

The woman nodded, her mouth full of sandwich. "A little," she said.

Rosemary sat herself in the chair opposite the woman. "I'm sure you do. I don't know how to do anything useful. I play the piano some. But I don't know who that's useful to." She laughed a little at her own remark. She wanted to ask her (out of curiosity and because later, when she told her friends about the girl she had helped, she wanted to be able to relate her story) how she had come to be in this circumstance. Surely, something terrible had happened to her, maybe more than one thing terrible, but she had escaped, she was all right now, she was safe. And there would be time to ask, she reasoned, after the tea and sandwiches had done their work and she was feeling refreshed.

Rosemary noticed there was a hole, more than one, in the girl's stockings and jumped up, not that she could ever sit for long, anyway. "I'll find you some stockings," she said and left the girl alone as she disappeared into the dressing room.

What she thought about while Rosemary was in the closet. The picture on the wall of the child sitting cross-legged in the woods with an angel overhead, an obvious hold-over from when Rosemary was young, the satin coverlet on the bed, the ivory and silver hairbrushes on the vanity, the warmth from the fire that made everything else seem so faraway. She hadn't realized how tired she'd been or how long it had been, not really that long, since she had sat down. Actually, a moment's peace.

"Try these," said Rosemary coming out of the closet with stockings and a skirt and a clean over-blouse. She didn't even have the heart to protest but rather let Rosemary press the clothes on her and show her into the bathroom.

Rosemary lit a cigarette and leaned against the mantel. Rosemary considered how she could phrase her inquiry, what she could ask to bring the girl out. Her temporary musing was broken by the door opening and a woman's voice.

"I hear you're on some kind of a tear." The woman who entered the room had a clipped way of speaking. Her clothes were plain and tailored but looked expensive. Her hair was cut unfashionably short. She seemed to take everything in in an instant. Her name was Jane Howard and she had been Rosemary's best friend since childhood and, from the way she entered the room, she had been doing this, entering without knocking, for some time.

Rosemary put a finger over her mouth to urge her to speak quietly. Jane looked around curiously. "What have you done?"

"I don't know quite," said Rosemary laughing. "It was an impulse. I met a girl. Well, I found her really."

"You—what?"

Rosemary stepped over to her and spoke softly. "Shh. Let me tell you. She was on a corner. She asked me for some money. And I thought—what if—well, you'll see her. What if circumstance, well, anyway, I thought what if I brought her home, gave her some clothes. God knows I have clothes I can spare. Helped her find a job somewhere. What if I actually made a difference. It would be so easy really."

"It's not that I don't commend you," said Jane, who privately thought people weren't quite like strays to be taken in so easily. "But have you thought about—" The way Rosemary stared at her stopped her mid-sentence.

"I couldn't resist it," said Rosemary. "I mean, think how I would feel if . . . I were actually able to help. What's the danger? Or, if there is one, doesn't that make it all the more exciting?" She laughed a little at herself. "Haven't you ever done anything on impulse," she asked, "just because you felt you should!"

"Well, of course, I have but—"

Their exchange was interrupted by the bathroom door opening and the object of their conversation stepping back into the room. The color had returned to her cheeks. The long, tangled hair was brushed now and her dark lips were quite full. She had deep, lighted eyes. The plain dark skirt, white shirt and sweater that had been pressed on her made her look almost as if she were one of them.

"Jane Howard," said Rosemary, "this is Miss—"

"Smith," said the girl. She stood there strangely still and unafraid. "Eleanor Smith."

"Charmed," said Jane Howard. But before they could have more of an interchange, the bedroom door opened again and Philip Alsop, Rosemary's fiancé, entered the room.

Eleanor studied him, although she was careful not to look at him too long, shyly dropping her eyes or turning back to Rosemary. She was unclear, at first, what his relation was to Rosemary. Brother? No, probably not, there wasn't enough of a physical resemblance. He was tall, good-looking with aristocratic lines, high cheekbones, but more substantial somehow, broad-shouldered with a slightly athletic countenance enhanced by the fact that his skin was tanned which

Eleanor mistakenly attributed to idle afternoons taken up with lawn tennis, boating, or whatever it was that gentlemen did on idle afternoons. But, really, it was from working on the docks as he owned a shipping business which he'd built up on his own. He was staring at her. She was used to that, men staring at her. What she wasn't used to was wanting to stare at them back.

"Rosemary, may I come in?" he said, somewhat after the fact. "Oh, I'm so sorry. I didn't realize you had— Oh, hi, Jane." He hadn't seen Jane at first because he was so struck by the appearance of Eleanor. There was something frail about the girl and yet exciting as if she had another side. Not like Rosemary's usual friends who were done up to appear exactly what they were. He looked at Rosemary questioningly.

"Philip, this is my friend Miss Smith. Eleanor Smith. We were just having tea. Would you like a cup, Philip? Jane?"

Philip shook his head, "No, I—"

Jane Howard interrupted. "I'll help myself as always," she said as she filled a plate with tea sandwiches and poured herself a cup of tea.

Philip had trouble taking his eyes off Eleanor even though he was speaking to Rosemary. "I was just going to ask you, Rose, to come into the library for a moment."

Rosemary laughed up at him. "I haven't done a thing about the wedding all day."

"It's not that," said Philip. "Actually, I can't wait until it's over. I don't mean that the way it sounds, but it is such a fuss for a single afternoon."

"Not such a fuss to start an entire life," said Rosemary smiling up at him.

Of course, thought Eleanor understanding, in that moment, their connection, he was her betrothed. She'd looked like a girl who had a perfect life.

"And you know," said Rosemary laughing, "how much I like to arrange things."

Philip smiled because he knew that every detail of the wedding mattered to her. "Would you excuse us, Jane? Miss Smith?" he asked looking once more at Miss Smith as he said it.

Rosemary answered for them. "Of course, they would." She followed Philip out of the room.

The rain was still beating steadily outside. Jane Howard walked over to the fireplace and took a cigarette off the mantel. She offered one to Eleanor. "Would you like one?" she asked.

Miss Smith narrowed her eyes. "I'd love one, thanks," she said almost languidly. And, in that moment, it appeared she might not be as innocent as she seemed.

$\mathscr{P}$hilip shut the door behind them to the library. "What gives?" he asked.

Rosemary came over and kissed him playfully on the mouth. "What do you mean, what gives?"

"Who *is* she?" Philip asked. "Where did you find her?"

"Could you tell, then?" said Rosemary laughing. "I picked her up."

Rosemary walked over to the fire. There was a mirror in a large wood frame behind them on the mantel. Rosemary looked at herself in the glass for a moment and at Philip standing behind her. She turned to him.

"That is what I did." She was sort of pleased with herself. It was like something in a Dostoyevsky story, to pick a girl up in the dusk and bring her home. "I found her on the corner of Greenwich," she said. "I don't know. You read about these things. And I just did it."

"And now what do you plan to do?" asked Philip. This wasn't the reaction she had expected. "You can't just pick someone up like that. And, then what?"

"I don't know," said Rosemary. "We haven't talked yet. Be nice to her. Be awfully nice to her. Show her—make her feel—"

Philip cut her off. "I'm not sure it can be done."

"Why not? . . ." said Rosemary, pouting again. "I want to. I decided—"

"She is so astonishingly pretty," he said.

"Pretty?" said Rosemary. "Do you think so? I hadn't thought of it." She turned and looked at her own face in the mirror for a moment. Philip looked at her reflection, as well.

"She's absolutely lovely," he insisted. "Take a look at her again." Rosemary turned to him. "I was knocked out by her when I came into your room just now. Even so, I think you're making a mistake." He laughed and said, "But let me know if Miss Smith is going to dine with us tonight."

Rosemary searched his face for a moment before she gave a small laugh back. "I will, Philip," she said.

osemary left the library but did not go immediately to her bedroom. She walked instead to the little sitting room upstairs where she kept her papers and wrote notes in the morning. Pretty! Absolutely lovely! I was knocked out by her when I walked into the room! She sat at the Victorian desk. Her cheeks were flushed. She reached for her chequebook. But cheques would be no use. She opened the desk drawer and took out fifteen one-dollar bills, and after a moment's contemplation, put three back, folded the others neatly and tucked them in the pocket of her skirt.

Eleanor and Jane were deep in conversation when she walked back into the room. Jane was laughing. Rosemary cut them off. "Jane, would you be a dear and check on Philip?"

Jane stubbed her cigarette out in the ashtray. "Of course," she said. Rosemary liked to run things in her own house and Jane Howard rarely questioned her. "It was awfully nice to have met you," she said to Eleanor, gave a small wave, and left the room.

Rosemary walked into the closet and hurriedly went through some things. She came out of the closet carrying an overcoat.

"I think the rain is stopping," she said to Eleanor.

Eleanor sat up on the couch. She knew what this meant.

Rosemary pressed the coat on her.

"No, take it," said Rosemary as the girl reached a hand up to protest. "I never wear the thing. It isn't new." Not that anything Rosemary had was old, probably only been worn a couple of times. "I've put some money in the pocket. No, don't say a word. If the tables were turned, you would—I wish I could do more."

Eleanor Smith just stared at her. She sat with the angled posture of a ballerina, slightly bemused, her head slightly tilted to one side, her hair falling perfectly around her face. She was not surprised that this had happened. She had almost a faint smile. She knew why she was being asked to leave.

"Are you sure you'll be all right?" asked Rosemary, wishing the girl would say anything and not just stare at her like that.

When she did answer, her voice was soft, extraordinarily composed and self-assured. "Yes, I'll be fine." She slipped the coat on over her shoulders. "Thank you—ma'am." The ma'am was almost an afterthought.

∽

Philip and Jane had switched to champagne when Rosemary walked into the library. She opened the door and leaned against the door frame and looked at them with her dazzled, exotic gaze. "Miss Smith," she said, "will not be joining us for dinner."

Philip looked surprised. "But," he said, "I thought—"

Jane Howard interrupted. "I can't stay either," she said, standing. "I've stayed too long already." Jane set her glass down on a table, blew a kiss with two fingers, and rushed out of the room.

After they left, the prospect of staying alone with Philip and filling the night up with simple conversation seemed too much for Rose. The air in the house felt thick as though something untoward had settled there. "Why don't we try that sweet little Italian place on the corner," she suggested, smiling up at Philip. "I don't feel like staying in."

It was just drizzling as Jane Howard hurried down the darkened street. She had no umbrella, just a hat, but she was not the sort to be bothered by the rain. She saw what she was looking for, the shape of a woman on the next block, and almost ran across the wet cobblestones which seemed to shimmer like cut glass.

"Wait!" she called out. "Miss Smith. I'm so glad to have caught you. It would have been terrible not to have seen you again."

Terrible not to have seen her again? Jane didn't give her an opportunity really to answer. She went on, "It's almost a pretty night out, if it wasn't so wet, that is. I always like the way it smells after a rain, don't you?" Jane continued to walk, long, mannish strides, so that Eleanor was forced to keep pace with her. "You might not like the way it smells after a rain. Not everyone does." This made Eleanor smile. There was something about the way Miss Howard rattled on. "I have a—I don't mean to intrude—but we have intruded, haven't we. Are you going to be all right?"

"I'll be fine," said Eleanor.

Jane Howard didn't look convinced. She stopped on the sidewalk unmindful of the rain which was coming down almost like a mist around them. She looked at Eleanor. "I have a friend," she said, "who owns a hat shop. Dora's, on Sutter. Here, I'll write it down for you. Tell her that I sent you, Jane, Jane Howard, and that I thought she might have a job for you. You'd be good at that, I think, selling hats." She smiled at Eleanor.

Eleanor was unsure what to make of this. She was not used to people taking care of her. This was what it was, then, to make a connection? To be given a helping hand? And, yet, it had a similar sting to when her mother had been forced to rummage shoes for her from the rector who'd always, after that, looked at her pityingly as if to say, her father can't even put shoes on her feet, would rather spend it on a Friday night at a local pub.

"I won't tell her anything about you," said Jane. "I'll leave that part up to you."

"Nothing is for free, Leni," her mother had said to her as they'd walked away from the parish, the new shoes snugly on her feet. "It's always best not to take something from someone, if you can help it. But there's some times when y'can't help it." But wasn't that the chance she was being given here, to work for a living, to have an honest job, to be dependent on no one but herself.

"Thank you," she said almost shyly. "I might stop by."

"Well, only if you think that it's a good idea," she said, having actually no idea what the girl did think. Jane Howard glanced at her watch. "I'm late," she said. Jane reached out her hand to say good-bye. "Good luck." And the interview ended as suddenly as it had begun, leaving Miss Smith again alone on a street corner.

There were confections of hats in the window. Hats with feathers, ribbons, and veils, everyday hats and hats for all occasions, celebratory hats and hats for mourning. It reminded Eleanor of when she was little and she used to stand outside the penny candy store on her corner, stare in the window, and wish she could go in and say, "I'll have one of everything." The man in the candy store used to give her sweets which was one of the first times she'd learned, when he'd coaxed her into the back of the store with the promise of a box of chocolates that he'd saved for her, that her mother didn't lie when she'd told her, "Nothing is for free,

Leni." He'd laughed when she pushed him away, laughed at what a silly girl she was. And then looked at her coldly and said, "But it's the only thing you have to barter with." After that, she would still allow herself to stop on the way home from school and look at the candy displayed in the window and sometimes she would stare at him, knowing that he would never dare to come out on the street and taunt her.

She entered the hat shop—shyly would be the wrong word, for she had too much poise to do anything shyly—but with a certain reserve.

Dora, the proprietress of the hat shop that bore her name, snatched a dark blue hat off a hatstand and glided over. "Oh, this will do nicely," she said as she set it expertly on Eleanor's head. She gently propelled her towards a mirror. "Oh, you don't like it?! Try this, then." She pulled a black hat with feathers off another hatstand and put it on Eleanor's head. "Daring? Bold!" She stepped back and surveyed her. "It certainly makes a statement. Don't you think?"

Eleanor still didn't answer her, just stared at herself in the mirror. "Not what you had in mind?" Dora snatched it off her head. "Try this." She pulled a little pink piece of fluff, like a pillbox, with a veil off a display and placed it daintily but firmly on Eleanor's head and fastened it with a hat pin.

Still no response. "You think it's too young for

you?!" She was trying very hard to get the girl to answer her. "Oh, well, you do have the face for it." She saw that Eleanor's eye was drawn to a very plain beige hat with a beautiful shape. "Oh, you like that one. Simple yet elegant." She took it off the handstand and handed it to Eleanor. "You try it."

Eleanor removed the pink hat from her head and gingerly placed it on a display case. She carefully set the beige one on her head and placed it at an angle. Her hair fell perfectly under it and her long pale neck and fine features were accentuated by its lines. She looked at herself in the mirror for a moment and turned to Dora meekly. "It's lovely." She was a little bit embarrassed at this next part, "Actually, I was looking for Dora," she said.

"The one and only. I hope you were looking for a hat."

Eleanor took the beige hat off her head and set it on top of a display case. She lowered her eyes. "No, I was looking for a job. I'm sorry." She took a step backwards, certain there was no job here. She hesitated. "Jane . . . Jane Howard sent me."

"And what did Miss Jane Howard think you could do?" asked Dora, studying the girl quite closely.

"She—she thought I might sell hats—I think."

"Well," said Dora, "you certainly can wear them. Do you have any experience? Of course, you don't.

You don't look like you have any experience at anything. How old are you?"

Eleanor's eyes got a little bit wider. "Twenty-four," she said.

"*How* old are you?"

"Twenty," she confessed.

"If you're any younger, I don't want to know. The hours are terrible. We open at eleven. You get here at nine. We close at six. Some nights from six to nine, we make hats, unless there's a wedding, in which case we work all night. You start tomorrow. Do you have any questions?"

Did this mean she had a job? It had all gone so quickly, she hadn't thought of anything to ask.

"You want to know what you're getting paid?" said Dora as though this ought to have been her first question. Before Eleanor could say anything, Dora answered this, as well. "Whatever I can afford. Some weeks, we do well, others . . ." She shrugged and shook her head and it was almost as though she was shaking her head for bringing the girl on, at all, given the off weeks. Dora picked up a purple felt piece she'd been shaping and started to sew. She didn't have any more questions. She didn't want to know too much about the girl; although she was curious in this case, she always felt it was better not to get too mixed up in her employees' lives, didn't want them coming to her for a handout or if their mother was sick, or they had a broken heart. Better to keep it polite and professional. "Keep the hat," she said almost dismissively, glancing over at the simple beige one Eleanor had left on the counter. "It suits you."

"Th-thank you," said Eleanor. She put the hat on her head and looked at herself in the mirror. And not knowing what else to say, she walked out the door.

Dora watched through the glass windows of the shop as Eleanor walked away down the street, her head tipped perfectly under her new beige hat. And, out loud, Dora said, to no one in particular, "And what else did Miss Jane Howard think you could do, I wonder?"

A sign on the door said: MISS WETZEL'S—BOARDING HOUSE FOR YOUNG LADIES. There was a pretzel vendor on the corner wearing a white cap and looking flushed from the heat of his pretzel stand. Eleanor walked over and bought herself a pretzel. She took a bite, savoring the taste of the salt on the warm dough. Down the street, a young boy hawking newspapers screamed out in an adolescent voice, "U.S. breaks diplomatic relations with Germany! Uncle Sam supports"—his voice went up on this—"European allies." And Eleanor was left to wonder whether he, too, would be sent to war next year. And whether three squares and the regimen wouldn't be good for him or, at least, only as hard as this.

It was starting to rain again. She stood and looked up at Wetzel's Boarding House. The curtains were grim and looked as though they could use a washing, the paint had chipped a bit on the facade but some of the best houses, not that this was one of them, had chipped paint. And certainly, she thought, it would do for now. She put her hand on the banister and started to mount the stairs.

At the top, she hesitated, then rapped the knocker. After a few moments, the door was opened by someone who was only a few years older than Eleanor but, on first glance, quite a bit more independent. Her name was Josie Kennedy and she had a full mane of brownish blond hair and a long-gaited walk that implied inbred confidence. "I wouldn't do that if I were you," said Josie.

"Do what?" asked Eleanor.

"Take one more step inside. Didn't your mother tell you? Terrible things happen to girls who take their lives into their own hands." She smiled at her. "I'm Josie Kennedy," she said. "On a good day, I am an actress." She posed—she put one hand against her head and slouched to the side. "Most of the time," she said, her voice dropping an octave as she straightened up again, "I work at Ted's, you know that little restaurant on Bank Street, one step up from a dive—but it's good for you because it means I bring home dinner and the tips are generally okay—which is where I'm headed now." Josie started to leave. "Tell Miss Wetzel you don't want meals except Sunday—Sunday, her sister cooks. You did want a room, didn't you?"

Eleanor nodded.

"What did you say your name was?"

"I—I didn't." There was a pattern here with these women for she'd felt that she could barely get a word in with any of them. "Eleanor. Eleanor Smith."

Josie repeated after her. "Eleanor. See you tonight." And Josie walked out into the night and left Eleanor standing in the doorway looking at the dark but cozy, in a modest, disheveled kind of way, interior of the house.

Miss Wetzel appeared at the top of the stairs. She was in her sixties, her hair in a bun with little stray white wisps flying about her forehead, her eyeglasses partly down her nose making her look even more severe and bird-like. "Did I hear someone knock?" she called out in a remarkably clear voice for someone her age.

Eleanor answered softly from the bottom of the stairs. "Yes, ma'am. It was me. Eleanor. Eleanor Smith. Miss Kennedy let me in."

Miss Wetzel cut her off. "Step into the light where I can see you," she said.

Eleanor did as she was told and stepped under the dim light of the hall so that she might be examined.

"Did you want a room?" Miss Wetzel asked.

"Yes, I did," said Eleanor.

Miss Wetzel studied her. Eleanor stood frozen in the entranceway until Miss Wetzel finally edged a few steps down the stairs. "Gas is included in the rent," she said, as she continued to descend.

Eleanor was uncharacteristically thrown by Miss Wetzel but it had been a remarkably long few days. "Yes, ma'am," she said again almost sheepishly.

"And meals." She peered at her up close now. "No gentleman callers after eight. And none upstairs ever. Where are your things?"

Eleanor hesitated. "I thought I would send for them later," she said.

Miss Wetzel shook her head. She didn't believe a word of this but she did have an empty room. She beckoned for Miss Smith to follow her upstairs.

*I*t wasn't the fur wrap around her shoulders that was keeping Rosemary warm, it was Philip's arms around her. The street was practically deserted. They were standing on the steps to her brownstone. They had been at the theatre and had a late supper afterwards at a café on Columbus that was frequented by a mixture of really important people . . . and writers and artists. Paul Lucien had announced, after two martinis, that he wanted to paint their portrait, causing Rosemary to wonder what such a thing would cost . . . and Philip had teased her that she wouldn't be able to sit that long. They'd had a bit to drink themselves, an awfully good claret and afterward cognac with their coffee. They were standing on the third step to her brownstone. He kissed her, playfully at first, and then it turned to something more urgent, something she could get lost in if she let herself. She felt his hand on her back through her dress. She moved slightly into him but then pushed him away.

She considered whether she should ask him in. He kissed her again and the force of it startled her. She pulled away when a carriage stopped unexpectedly a few houses away. She looked at Philip and smiled and he kissed her again. For a moment, she responded but then pulled back again.

"Stop it, Philip," she said. "It's late."

"You don't really want me to stop," he said. He buried his face in the soft curve of her breasts. He started to kiss her there.

"We're running out of time, Rose," he said so quietly it made her hold her breath. He meant the war, the thing they never spoke about. And that there were rumours that the U.S. might soon join.

"Don't say that, Philip," Rosemary answered. "It frightens me."

He looked at her and smiled sadly. His Rosemary, who never had a hair, a button out of place, who stepped so easily out of her car into the warmth of wherever she was going. In a way, she was as innocent as a child. She seemed to live her life as though she honestly believed that nothing bad would ever happen, and, if were to, by sheer force of will, she thought she would be able to right it. It was one of the things he admired most about Rosemary, that she staunchly believed that things should be a certain way . . . and that she had the luxury to believe it. "Oh, my precious, Rosemary," he said, stroking her hair softly, "in her almost perfect world."

*T*he city felt as though it had been washed clean, the rain had finally stopped entirely, and the air was full with the fragrant smell of the onset of spring. Rosemary had been out for a walk, a constitutional so to speak, uncharacteristically without a store as a destination.

She took her hat off and shook her hair out as she walked into the library where her father was sitting in a leather chair listening to news of the war on the radio. She had color from the outdoors. She looked almost pretty. Henry Fell hardly noticed she'd come in, intent as he was on hearing the news from Europe.

That was all anyone did anymore was listen to news

of Europe and speak about the war. "Will you think I'm terrible," asked Rosemary petulantly, "if I tell you that I'm sick of Archduke Ferdinand?"

Her father chided her softly. "Are you going to tell me that you're sick of the Archduchess Sophia, too?" he asked. He was teasing but trying to elicit a more human response, for although history would forget this, the Archduchess was killed alongside her husband and whatever Rosemary's mood, she had always been a defender of women.

"No," she answered soberly, "but their legacy lives after them. I don't want to hear about Bismarck or how they feel in France." Her father switched off the radio and looked at her carefully. She looked back at him. Her voice softened. "I would just like one day," she said, "where I didn't feel as though the world, my world, was in, was about to be in, a state of siege . . ."

Mr. Fell stared at his daughter and wondered whether he'd raised her at all adequately for any of the things she had to deal with now. But do we ever raise our children, particularly those as pampered and protected as Rose has been, to deal with whatever unexpected occurrences life throws at them? "What," Mr. Fell wondered, "defined character and backbone?" What lessons had he passed on about morality and perseverance? He looked at his daughter's unlined face, his child who had known little of tragedy except her mother's death and she was so young when that occurred.

"No," he said, "I don't think you're terrible. I just think you want the war to end."

Rosemary stood by the fireplace, an almost wistful expression on her face, framed like a cameo by the flickering light of the fire behind her. She looked for a moment like what she was, a society girl who had lost the society she was raised in.

When Jane Howard came over for her practically regular afternoon visit, she found Rosemary up in her bedroom, the canopied bed scattered with pieces of lace, samples, for her veil and wedding dress and train. Rosemary looked displeased. Jane set aside a pile of lace, cleared a spot for herself, and sat on the edge of the bed. Rosemary sorted through a number of the pieces and held up a square of pure-white netted lace with curlicues of butterflies and daisies, clearly hand-made as the pattern was irregular. "I think it's a little fussy, don't you?" she said and put it down again without waiting for Jane to answer her.

She picked up a darker piece with a simpler pattern almost like a spider's web and a slightly brownish hue. She stared at it for a moment and shook her head. "Antique white?!" she said with some disdain. "This is beige. Antique white should just be old not brown, slightly yellow as though it's been passed down."

"This should be your biggest problem in your marriage . . ." said Jane who thought the enterprise of picking lace a fairly ridiculous one, anyway.

Rosemary sat down next to her and took her hand. "Just today, let's make it my biggest problem." She dropped her hand as suddenly as she'd taken it, jumped up, and started to walk around the room. "Or what we're going to have for lunch. Do you think you would want fish? It's almost hot today. Or should we just have salad? Or could my biggest problem be what I'm going to wear tonight?"

She walked over and picked up a dress that was draped across a chair. It was a silk dress cut low in the bodice with tiny sleeves that went right off the shoulder. Collar lines were plunging that spring and dresses were becoming more revealing. Rosemary held it up against her. "What do you think of this?" she asked. "Is it too bare? I'm not sure I have a corset small enough to fit under it." Her voice dropped. "He's enlisted."

"What?!"

"Philip. He's told me that he's going off to war."

Did they really think that none of this was going to touch them?

"When—?"

"They've said they'll hold his orders until two days after the wedding. Of course, we'll have to move the wedding up." Rosemary laughed and shook her head. She suddenly looked tired. "Why couldn't he have just said he had essential service here?"

Jane looked at her sadly. Did any of them know, really, what the next few years was going to bring. "Philip's not like us, Rose."

Philip Alsop's father had died when he was fairly young and not left him and his mother well provided for. Philip had always gone to the best schools somehow, but had always been the poorest boy in them. There had always been the money owed to the butcher, the dressmaker, the tailor. It was part of his mother's talent to get them to continue to extend credit but it took its toll on her. It had made him stronger though, more determined, more responsible. He'd started with a storefront on the docks and built his shipping business up himself. "Unlike the rest of us," said Jane, "he's worked for everything he has. It isn't an indictment, Rose. It's just a fact."

"What does that mean?" asked Rosemary. "That

he has a different sense of duty than the rest of us. I intend to volunteer."

"Of course you do, dear," said Jane soothingly. Better not to have a fight. Rosemary always thought her positions were correct, exemplary. Rosemary probably thought that she was "essential service" here. Poor Rose. Did she really think the war wouldn't change anything at all?

"Two days . . ." said Rosemary, picking up another piece of lace. "We can't go away. Should we check into the Plaza for a night . . ." She was half-joking when she added, "Or just take a ferry around Staten Island?"

*E*leanor didn't understand why Jane Howard thought she would be good at this. These women had no idea what they wanted half the time and they didn't trust anyone else to tell them what looked good. And, to further complicate the enterprise, Eleanor had discovered that her sense of aesthetics was so strong that she couldn't let anyone out of the shop wearing a hat that *didn't* flatter them. Somehow, she justified it, that wouldn't be good for business, anyway.

On the afternoon in question, a society woman named Emily Mayhew had wandered into the shop in search of a hat for her daughter's commencement, with her daughter, the thirteen-year-old object of the commencement, Caitlin Mayhew, in tow. They were accompanied by a small brown terrier by the name of Tiger who went everywhere with them and a woman friend of Mrs. Mayhew's who appeared to have more interest in gossiping than in hats, although she occasionally interrupted their discourse to make disparaging remarks about any number of them.

Eleanor first tried a navy hat on Mrs. Mayhew's head that was oval shaped with a brim that arched slightly over her forehead.

"I don't know . . ." said Mrs. Mayhew, looking in the mirror.

"It makes your nose look too long," said her friend.

Eleanor said sweetly, "I think you have a nice nose."

"Patrician," said Mrs. Mayhew cutting her off. She turned back to her friend. "*Anyway*, they're all smitten with her. Under her spell, I should say." Mrs. Mayhew laughed at her own joke. "I think she has an odd name for a seer, 'Madame Olga'!" The woman she was referring to was a psychic, a gypsy, who recently, because of a number of well-placed predictions, had become a bit of a rage about town. "Katherine swears she conjured up Henry Goggins the other night right in Mrs. Van der Owen's living room," said Mrs. Mayhew. "But why they would want to conjure up Henry Goggins is beyond me."

"I sort of liked him," said Mrs. Mayhew's friend, Hilary.

"Hilary!" said Mrs. Mayhew as though her friend had said something untoward. The two of them giggled. Caitlin looked bored, awkward, slumped in her chair in a perfect teenage adolescent slouch.

"But I was thinking," said Mrs. Mayhew, "what if I could talk to Mama! I always wanted to know what happened to that ruby brooch. Look around, Caitlin. You have to do this, too. It is *your* commencement."

Caitlin looked completely disinterested in the idea of a new hat.

"You know that Daddy wants you to look nice," said Mrs. Mayhew and turned back to her friend. "Not that he'll notice. Theodore doesn't notice anything. I am trying to get him to spend less time at his club. Not that that will matter. What is it that makes a man so distracted even when he's with you?! I talk—he doesn't hear a word I say."

Mrs. Mayhew glanced over at a lighter, fluffier, extremely floral hat on a display.

Eleanor snatched it up. "Try it, Mrs. Mayhew," Eleanor suggested almost timidly.

"Oh dear, no," said Mrs. Mayhew. "I'd look like a landing strip for birds." And without losing a beat, she turned back to Hilary again and continued chatting. "Not that I think he should care what color the curtains are, but when I redo the entire bedroom, at least he could notice. I bet if Henry Goggins were to materialize in the bedroom, he wouldn't even notice that."

Mrs. Mayhew turned to her daughter. "You couldn't find one either, could you, Caitlin?" Mrs. Mayhew stood, obviously done with the shop and ready to move on. Eleanor panicked. They were suddenly a test of whether she could do this. She pulled a dove gray felt hat from a drawer. "No, wait," she said, "I'll design one for you." And then her voice got softer. "*Just* for you. No one in New York will have anything like it."

Intrigued, Mrs. Mayhew sat down again. Eleanor placed the hat on her head and tipped it at an angle. "See, it suits you. Plain, simple lines. Elegant. See, it hits your forehead, just so." She rummaged through a drawer and found a feather and a darker beige hatband. She put the feather on the side at an angle and secured it with the hatband. Mrs. Mayhew's short bobbed hair curled out from just under the rim.

Mrs. Mayhew stared at herself in the mirror critically. "No, I like it," she said. She stood up, the hat still on her head like a beacon. "Why didn't you just do that to begin with?"

Eleanor smiled politely and turned her attention to Mrs. Mayhew's daughter. "Now, let's see what you want."

Caitlin Mayhew looked at her sullenly.

"Is there *anything* you like?" asked Eleanor.

Caitlin pulled a large, plain black hat from a display stand.

"Caitlin!" her mother admonished her. "You can't wear a black hat to your commencement."

Caitlin put a hand over her forehead and slumped back into her chair.

"I could design something for you, too," said Eleanor, careful not to sound too enthusiastic.

Caitlin looked at her skeptically. Eleanor pulled a light chocolate brown wide-rimmed sun hat from a shelf and a yellow ribbon from a drawer. She looked at Caitlin and smiled, and it was clear that she would win this, too.

And, finally, Dora had to admit that Eleanor did have a knack for selling hats. She had confessed to Dora that she'd learned a bit of sewing as a child. "There wasn't anyone else to do the mending," she'd explained which was about all she had explained. Her hands seemed to take naturally to the finer part, delicate stitches, embroidery. She knew the right way, instinctively, to set a bead on a piece of lace, the perfect shade of ribbon for each hat, yet often such unusual choices. She had a good eye for design, subtle, nothing obvious or gauche. And, odder still, she was seemingly honest, which was strange, since she really had come in off

57

the street although by what means, Dora still didn't realize.

After awhile, Dora began to take more time to herself, longer lunches, naps at home when she'd had more than a glass of wine, an occasional afternoon liaison. She instructed Eleanor, "Just do the sewing in the front whenever I'm out, that way you can keep an eye on who comes in. And, if you feel like it, wear anything in the shop. As if you're a bit of an ad."

It was on just such an afternoon, when Dora was out on an errand or rather, lying prone at home, when Eleanor was sitting, a bit like a picture in the window, with her head bowed intently sewing a ribbon on a hat, when the bells on the shop door jingled and a man entered in uniform.

She finished her stitch and looked up at him. She recognized Philip Alsop at once. The uniform made a difference, made him look more solid somehow, not that she hadn't thought he was attractive when she first met him but she'd pegged him as one of those rich, flighty types. She studied him. She wondered what it would be like to be in his world all the time.

"Hello," he said, "I'm supposed to pick up Miss Fell's hats," he said and smiled. There was a dimple evident just below his right cheekbone. There was something kind about his eyes, yet serious, as though he'd seen things, knew things, was somehow deeper than he'd first appeared. The muscles in his arms were well-defined. She was aware that they were alone in the hat shop.

"Yes," said Eleanor, "I knew someone was coming."

It was the voice that tipped him. He remembered her voice. It was oddly cultured, yet direct, as though she could defend herself if pushed. He was as taken with her as the first time he'd seen her.

He stared at her. After a moment, he said, "It is you, isn't it?"

She nodded, "Yes, I'm afraid it is."

He teased her. "Afraid of me?" he said.

Uncomfortable with the familiarity, she didn't answer him. She shook her head. Then felt the need to put a proper amount of distance between them. "Let me get you your—Miss Fell's hats."

"It's such a surprise to see you here," he called out to the back room, but it was Dora who'd returned from lunch who came out of the back room bearing the many hat boxes.

"Oh—" said Philip, catching himself, as Dora started to gush at him. "You've come for the wedding hats. It's been such a rush."

"Yes, of course it has," he said.

"The war . . . I don't think we've ever worked this quickly," said Dora making an odd face. "Although, if you ask me," she added, "it's about time we went over there."

"Yes, ma'am, of course it is," said Philip.

"And then she kept adding things—"

Philip laughed. "She always does that. That's why I wouldn't let her come today. I was afraid she would change something else. Do I owe you something?" he asked.

"Oh, no," said Dora, shaking her head, "I've put it on her account."

Eleanor walked back into the shop from the workroom carrying even more hat boxes. She said, as she would to anyone who had come into the shop, "I can help you with these to the car." And then, aware of Dora's watchful gaze, she straightened and added, "There are certainly too many for you to carry."

Dora opened the shop door for them, and looked after them curiously as they walked to the car.

"How are you?" asked Philip as they walked to his car.

Eleanor, suddenly shy, didn't answer.

"I can see how you are," he said. "You're fine."

She smiled at this.

"Better than the last time I saw you, anyway," said Philip.

"Certainly better than that," she said.

Eleanor and Philip approached his car, juggling the

many hat boxes. "I'd hoped that she was coming in," said Eleanor. "I wanted to—"

Philip interrupted, "Thank her?"

"No, I wanted her to see me. I should thank her."

She helped him load the hat boxes into the back of the car. One of the boxes she was carrying flew from off of the top of the others. She leaned over to catch it as Philip did the same and caught it just before it hit the ground. The effect of it was the two of them were pressed together. She set the hat boxes down on the pavement and took a breath.

"I wanted to see you," he said very softly. Her face was framed in reflection in the back window of the car. She was so very pretty. Her clothes were simple, almost elegant. She looked a long way from the street.

Dora, who was sitting at the front table doing paperwork, looked out the window and thought she saw him lean down and whisper something in Eleanor's ear.

It was almost dark out when they closed up for the night. Eleanor seemed in a hurry but stayed and helped as Dora fluttered fitfully about the shop methodically and meticulously removing the hats from the hatstands and putting them away in drawers as she did each evening.

"I can never sleep when I've finished a job like this," said Dora. 'You'd think it would be during. That I'd be so nervous how they'd turn out that I couldn't sleep. But for me, it's after. I've given them the hats and . . ." She gestured with her hand. "They never invite us to the wedding, you know."

Dora tucked another hat in a drawer after wrapping it carefully in tissue paper and closed the drawer more forcefully than necessary. "Not that I think much of her," she said, "or her hats for that matter. As Henry James once said about one of his characters"—she gave a little bit of a laugh—" 'Her imagination is bounded on the East by Madison Avenue.' And she doesn't think anyone else can *have* an opinion." Dora placed another hat in a drawer. "I'm off to my sister's," she said. And then in a completely different tone of voice added, "You open tomorrow. We should do well. It's spring. Not that it matters. We've done well enough this spring, thanks to the war. I wonder, if it were in our backyard, if we would be so festive."

There was a carriage parked on the corner of the street. If Dora had not chosen to go out the back door she probably would have seen Eleanor arrive at the corner and Philip Alsop reach from inside the car and open the passenger side door.

It had simply been his intention to offer her a ride home. He did not intend to take her for a drink. He did not think he was going to kiss her. There was something about her that made him want to take care of her a little. Eleanor was shy, hesitant, at first, that she ought not to accept a ride with him

63

but he insisted. She stepped into the carriage. Her face was lit softly from the streetlight. He took her gloved hand in his to help her in and all the other things occurred to him. He did not immediately let go of her hand.

*H*ad she had too many glasses of champagne so that time seemed almost frozen, slower than usual, sound oddly amplified, as men on the other side of the room whispered about liaisons and stock prices and whatever men whispered about in a room like this. The cigarette girl paused in front of her. Rosemary declined. She was feeling too light-headed to smoke. The restaurant was dimly lit and on a very high story of the building, with large windows so that the city was visible outside, the skyline etched in shadow, almost minimalist, jaggedly beautiful, with the row of brownstones and the river visible just beyond. She was acutely aware of a

woman on the other side of the room laughing, sur-
rounded by three admiring men, punctuated by the
black piano player, Charlie Miles, whom she'd known
since she was a child, crooning a song about love. It
wasn't like Philip to be late. She felt strangely un-
guarded as though a layer had been stripped away and
one look at her face would reveal the anxiousness she
felt. She forced a smile and walked over to the piano.
She set her champagne glass down on the top of the
piano, and Charlie broke into an instrumental and began to speak to her about the other people in the room,
specifically a couple dancing on the dance floor.

"He thinks she's in love with him," Charlie said to
her under his breath, "but if you could have seen her
last night with Freddy Bagley . . ."

"Yes," Rosemary laughed, "but *she* has no repu-
tation to protect." He still hadn't arrived. Should she
take a seat at a table and order herself dinner and
pretend that he'd told her he was going to be delayed?
She took a sip of champagne and started to feel a little
less at sea. And then a man's hand was on her back.

"I'm sorry I'm so late." It was Philip. "I got your
hats. I was"—he hesitated, "at the War Office . . ."
Rosemary looked at him questioningly. "At least I
haven't missed dinner," he said. "And you, I trust"—
he looked gratefully at Charlie Miles—"have been

66

well entertained." He put his arm casually on her shoulder.

Did she expect him to remark on her dress or the line of kohl under her eyes that made her eyelashes look longer than usual? Did she expect him to be knocked out by her when he walked into the room. Am I pretty, Philip?

It was a few days later that Rosemary was sitting at her desk
opening her mail with the silver letter opener that
she'd purchased from Mr. Rhenquist. Philip was lying
on his back on the couch with his feet up on the arm
of the sofa. "I should go to the Foundling Hospital's
annual tea," she said opening yet another invitation.
"Will you go with me?"

"Oh, Rose, do I have to?"

She didn't answer him because she had immediately
opened another letter and was distracted by its contents. A sort of florid card, one you would buy at a

dimestore, not the usual engraved stationery. She opened the card which had a note written on it and some money stuffed inside it.

"I hate it when you don't answer me," he said. "Is this what I have to look forward to—years and years as a neglected . . . husband?"

Rosemary interrupted him. "Philip, she's sent me back my money."

He knew instantly who she meant.

"I never expected her to repay me," Rosemary said. "Do you remember that girl I picked up?"

"Who?" he said, appearing to still be distracted.

"You know. Miss Smith. The one I picked up that day in the rain and brought home for tea. Do you think maybe I helped her?" Rosemary looked very pleased with herself.

On the couch, Philip has shut his eyes.

The shops were closing for the night. The streets were crowded with taxis, carriages, people on their way home on foot or running to catch the streetcar, women with children hanging on their skirts making hurried stops in food-stores and the apothecary shop on the corner which closed conveniently a half-hour after everyone else.

The street lamps were just coming on as Eleanor came out of the hat shop and found Philip's carriage parked on the corner. He'd let his driver go and was holding the reins of the two chestnut mares himself, a driver's cap pulled down over his forehead. Despite it, she recognized him at once. He'd rolled the window down as if he were waiting for her. "Did we have an appointment?" she asked him.

"No," he said, "I wanted to see you." He smiled at her and she remembered again how charming he was but it didn't deter her.

"Oh. And I'm here whenever you want to see me. In between the other things?" She started to walk away from him down the crowded street.

Did he think she was going to be easy? No, if he'd thought that, he wouldn't have been interested in her.

He started to follow her in the carriage. "You're making a scene," he said, casually, as if he were amused by her.

"*I'm* making a scene?"

He smiled again.

"Don't you care?" she asked him, surprised that he would take a chance like this.

"I just thought we could have dinner," he said as politely as he could.

"Actually have dinner. I actually have other plans."

"Another time, then," he said. He closed the window and the carriage took off down the street. And then as abruptly as this began, it ended. It wasn't clear who'd won this exchange.

He didn't feel like going to his club where there would certainly be talk of war. He directed his driver instead to take him to Jane Howard's.

$\mathcal{J}$ ane Howard and Philip Alsop had been friends since they were children, since before Philip's father died. She remembered when he lived in the big house on the corner of 9th Street and Fifth Avenue, when he wore short pants and had a pony of his own, when his mother was still beautiful before the hardships of her life ravaged her once unlined face.

He had always confided in her, never questioned her loyalty to him and with good reason, as Jane had always been the person in his (and Rosemary's) life whom they told their darkest secrets to, and she, in turn, had incited them to do things she would never have done herself. They had the kind of comfort with each other that cousins had, a mischievous conspiratorial streak from too many unchaperoned hours when they were children and the grown-ups were busy doing whatever grown-ups did on idle summer afternoons and evenings.

Jane was standing at the mantel with her back to the room smoking a cigarette. Philip was lying on the couch. She had offered him wine which he declined preferring something stronger, whiskey neat, and was on his second glass.

"It's like an addiction," he said with some excitement and a small degree of distress.

Jane turned to him and took a long draw on her cigarette. "She has that effect. Certainly on me."

Philip looked at her as though they had a mutual understanding.

"Don't look at me like that," she said. "But I *was* compelled to follow her that night. She looked as if no one had ever taken care of her. I—sent her to Dora."

"So, I have you to blame," he said.

Jane raised an eyebrow, amused, unmindful of the consequences all of it might have.

It was late at night when Eleanor, certainly innocent that she'd been the object of any conversation, walked down the street with Josie Kennedy. The two of them had been at a late dinner after the theater and had a couple of drinks with a few friends of Josie's, a fairly innocent night all in all. As they approached the dreaded Wetzel's boarding house (as they sometimes called the dear woman behind her back), Philip was standing on the corner under a streetlight. He looked completely relaxed, as though he had nothing better to do than stand on the street corner enjoying the night air.

Eleanor was annoyed because it was starting to feel

like an intrusion. She had come out of the shop that afternoon and found Philip's carriage parked on the corner—as though she should be there at his whim! He *was* engaged and she was beginning to feel like something he was toying with.

Josie stood awkwardly a few feet away. Eleanor made no effort to introduce them.

"I'll see you at home, then," Josie said after an awkward moment.

Eleanor nodded at her and continued to look at Philip. She had some responsibility here. Yes, she had accepted a ride from him, stopped for a drink, and then, feeling the effects of the champagne, had kissed him goodbye but had meant it to be that, a kiss goodbye. It had been a mistake. Did he think she would be so flattered by the attentions of any man like him? That there was something more to this?

"I didn't think this was your neighborhood," she said finally.

"I don't deserve that."

Eleanor wondered what he thought he did deserve or what right he thought he had to be on her corner. "Are you following me?" she asked him.

"No, I was waiting for you." He smiled at her again but there was something in the way he stood, a respectful distance from her, as though he were asking this time.

"I wish I could do this the right way," he said. "I don't have time. I wish I did. If I had time, it—could be different. If I could make an appointment and take you to dinner next week. I don't feel I have control of this, Eleanor . . ." His voice trailed off. "Any day I could get my orders. And leave for Europe."

"And I'd be here," she said almost without inflection.

He stepped in closer and put his hand on her hair. Her inclination was to fall into him. She stopped herself.

He leaned in and kissed her and the only thing she could do was kiss him back. He led her by the hand to his carriage. But it was never clear with them who was doing the leading.

The dining room table was elaborately set for one with long ivory candles burning in the imposing silver candelabra. Rosemary's father, Henry Fell, was sitting alone at the head of the long table reading one of his many reference books and occasionally, absentmindedly taking a sip of consommé from a silver soupspoon, unmindful of the fact that it had grown cold many minutes before. The mahogany doors to the dining room slid open and his daughter glided dramatically into the room. "You'll have to put your book away, Papa, if you want to eat with me," she said and kissed him on the forehead. She sat down next to him at the table.

"And what makes you think I prefer you to my present companion?" he asked teasing, then smiled at her and shut the book although he didn't trust this sudden attention. "And why is my sweetheart home, tonight?"

"Oh, I didn't think we'd been spending enough time together, did you?"

Henry Fell raised an eyebrow. "And where is Philip?"

"Playing cards—I think."

Rosemary got up and helped herself to an empty soup bowl from the sideboard, a napkin, and a necessary selection of silver. She didn't actually know where Philip was that night. Had they made plans? She couldn't actually remember. She sat back down at the table and took the top off the soup tureen. "Is this all we're having for dinner?" She made a face. "Dull, brown liquid?"

"Oh, Rosemary. Don't start with Gertrude."

"Oh, Papa, she likes it." Rosemary smiled at him impishly. She picked up the silver bell on the table and rang for Gertrude to come from the kitchen. And though she might not be able to control the rest of her life, it was clear she was going to have whatever she wanted for dinner.

Not so many blocks away, the city was dark as the carriage flew towards Philip's house. There was an antic, urgent quality to the night as though a collective insanity had gripped the city and all through-out it there were women in the company of men who they knew that they might never see again.

Eleanor would remember every moment of that night as though it were etched in glass, indelibly. How many stairs there were to his front door, nine, that one light was on in the parlor by the leather chair where she imagined that he sometimes read, that the fifth stair on the staircase leading up to his rooms had a slight crack as though at some point it had suffered water damage . . . and the carpet was fairly worn at the landing, once a deep purple color that had faded to gray.

That his bedroom was much less grand than she had imagined it to be. There were no words as he undid the many tiny buttons of her blouse and then her corset in his bedroom. She looked completely trusting—as though her whole life had been about this moment. The room was barely lit by a gas sconce and the reflected light of a street lamp from outside as they lay fluid in each other's arms, naked on the bed, as though they belonged together, and, for that moment at least, there was nothing else in the world.

The next morning, Philip opened his eyes and barely focussed. The bedroom was flooded with sunlight. He put one hand over his eyes to shade them and with his other reached for Eleanor next to him in the bed. But she was already up, bathed, and dressing in the corner of the room with her back to him. He tried to convince her to come back to bed. But she insisted that she had to go to work.

"I'll have my driver take you," he said.

She finished the sentence for him. ". . . And drop me four blocks away, so nobody will see."

He sat up in bed and put a pillow behind his head. He looked chastened. He wasn't sure how to respond to her.

"It's one thing in the night," she said, "but in the daytime when everyone can see and our eyes aren't tricked by shadows or artificial light . . ."

"Don't make me feel cheap, Eleanor. It's not something I would ever do to you. Take the day off. I'll take it, too."

"That's easy for you," she said. "You work for yourself," reminding him again of the differences between them.

"We'll send a note in that you're ill," he said and smiled. And in that moment, she realized that she wasn't just an evening's entertainment. Almost without meaning to, she'd crossed the room and his arms were around her once again.

It was long after the customary time for breakfast when they finally went out onto the street and stopped in a bakery for fresh buns and warm cups of tea. Philip took her downtown and they walked the open air markets on Canal Street. He bought a basket of fresh apricots. Eleanor took a bite of one, warm from the sun, and a bit of juice dripped down her chin. He reached his hand over to clean her face and she held his hand

and kissed it. They stopped at a stand of silks where he bought a shawl for her that was wildly over-priced but, under the circumstances bartering would never occur to him. She wrapped it around her shoulders. He took the edges of the shawl where it lightly fringed and wrapped them around his back, as well, binding them together. And then, leaned in and kissed her. They were so far from his normal, social world that it didn't occur to him that anyone would see them.

The mood at Rosemary's was much the same as always. The champagne flowed easily, the slight clink of glasses from good crystal, despite the fact that the guests toasted one another for a future that for the first time was uncertain. There were plates of hors d'oeuvres passed on silver platters. There was a discussion on one side of the room about a play that was all the rage on Broadway but that Rosemary's friend Sarah found baffling. "They made such a fuss about it in the *Times*," said Sarah, "and then we went to see it . . . ? Maybe I'm not much for, what do they call it, satire?"

"I liked it," her husband said.

"Of course you did, dear," she said and looked at him rather patronizingly until he added, "Maybe your problem is that we are the thing that is being satirized."

"I think I'll skip it," said Rosemary more in an effort to placate Sarah than to miss an experience. "Can I offer you a little more champagne?"

Rosemary's father stuck his head in for a moment and decided he'd rather not be part of this gathering, at least for the moment. He helped himself to a toast with salmon and retired, presumably, to his study.

Jane and Philip were standing by the window which was framed by heavy velvet drapes. They were talking softly, almost conspiratorially.

"You've seen her?" Jane asked but it was more a statement than a question. And there was a look on his face which made it all seem not so light anymore, not something simply to be dabbled in. "Are you sure you haven't taken on more than you can . . ."

He put a hand on her arm and tried to stop her but she continued questioning him.

"Are you feeling a certain amount of guilt?" Jane asked.

He came right back at her. "Are you?"

They didn't notice Rosemary was standing there

until she spoke. "Do either of you need another drink?" And then, because Jane looked so startled, Rosemary said, "Oh, I've interrupted you."

"No," said Jane, a little bit too quickly, "we were just discussing the pressures of war on modern society."

"A subject I'm familiar with but would rather not discuss," said Rosemary. She gave Philip a kiss on the cheek and went off to tend to her other guests.

"A certain amount of guilt," said Philip after she was a safe distance away. "Yes, I would say that."

It was hard to tell what the aged Miss Wetzel thought of her charges, if they could indeed be called that. Certainly, if you asked her, the nature of the individual girls she'd boarded in the last ten years had become as a whole markedly wilder and more independent. No one ever stayed there very long. Wetzel's was a stopping place. But except for an occasional stern reprimand when one of the house rules was broken, Miss Wetzel mostly kept to herself, retiring at half past eight each night to her lonely bed and the few pages of the Bible, New Testament only, she read before retiring. The girls treated the house more like a boarding school, preferring to do their living in their rooms instead of in the bleak and modest parlor downstairs. And once Wetzel fell asleep, as she could barely hear when awake, they felt it would take a near avalanche to rouse her.

Eleanor liked the simplicity of Wetzel's. Most nights she stayed in. It had been so long since she'd felt safe anywhere. Since childhood when she'd had to dodge her father's drunken rages that could turn so easily to maudlin self-pity (which was somehow even harder for her to bear)—she'd always felt as though she'd been on her own. She would take a bit of work home from the shop some nights. On the night in question, she was sitting at the vanity in her room, wearing the silk shawl that Philip had bought for her wrapped around her shoulders, imitating the casual nature of two women who were in the shop that day, running Dora fairly ragged but spending. They were not her usual sort of customers, as Dora seemed to specialize in *Old New York*. These were women who had married well, blonde with perfectly made-up faces. They were women who had invented themselves successfully, as if they themselves were something to be marketed, and they shopped the way a child would shop, unbridled in a toy store.

"I'll have one of those," said the first woman pointing to an elegant forest green hat with a veil as if there were many of them sitting somewhere on a shelf. "Oh," she added as if it had just occurred to her, "and I need a navy blue hat."

Dora obligingly showed her one which was instantly accepted, rather than scrutinized, as if she didn't realize if she were to reject it, two or three other styles would magically appear.

Eleanor stood in the doorway of the workroom watching them, silently studying their moves.

The second woman, who looked very much like the first woman except that she was a few inches taller, spoke in a voice that was a little husky and fairly trilled with laughter. "I like that little white one," she said. She picked up a fluffy concoction with a veil and held it in front of her. She didn't even try it on. "Of course, I couldn't wear it till the spring," she said. "But it will keep."

Eleanor picked up a white straw summer hat she had been stitching and put it on her head. She looked at herself in the mirror of the vanity. She secured it to her head with a hat pin and said out loud as she looked at herself in the mirror, "Of course, I couldn't wear it till the spring, but it will keep."

Her reverie was broken by a knock at the door, a very quiet tapping but insistent. She hurriedly unpinned the hat as though afraid she would be caught playing at something she ought not to be playing at and opened the door a crack. It was Philip. Eleanor spoke to him in a half-whisper. "You shouldn't be here." House rules—no male visitors. It was almost a game to her. She pretended every night that it was the first time he'd come to see her, as though she needed to preserve some vestige of prudery before she let him in the door. And then his immediate response, "But you're glad I am. Let me in before I make a scene."

After she'd shut the door, "You're always threatening to make a scene," she said. She put a finger to her mouth. She was almost laughing. "Shh. You'll get me thrown out of here."

He leaned in and kissed her. There was no need after that to quiet him.

Philip didn't spend the night, he left at three in the morning. Eleanor stood in the window watching him as he walked out of the building onto the street. She was wearing a silk robe, her hair was down, her face reflected in the pane of glass, and she looked as innocent as if she were fourteen. He'd brought her a present that night, a necklace that had belonged to his mother, a delicate chain of white gold and at the base of it a small inlay of diamonds around a larger square-cut diamond, elegant and simple although the middle stone was quite impressive. He told her, his father had given it to his mother the month before they married and it was the one piece that she had refused to pawn.

She put her hand on the diamond. *It was his mother's and he'd given it to her.* . . .

She watched as, on the street, Philip got into his carriage. He half-turned when he was on the step of the running board, almost inside, and looked up at her. She put a hand to her face and stood there watching as he got in and the carriage took off down the street.

The next morning, Eleanor was rearranging the hats on display, all light colored and pastel because it was spring, jauntily tipping them at angles on their stands. Dora was sitting behind the desk, practically immobile as she was most mornings, drinking a cup of coffee that Eleanor had brought for her from the café across the street and looking at the morning paper. Dora opened the newspaper and flipped immediately to the Society Page.

"You can't buy publicity like this," she said, suddenly excited, as she spread the newspaper out on the table. "She's wearing our hat! See, I do give you credit, dear," she said to Eleanor.

She read the item aloud:

"Miss Rosemary Fell and Captain Philip Alsop will be wed . . ."

She was only glad her back was turned so that Dora couldn't see her face.

". . . A month earlier than planned. At St. Luke's Cathedral tomorrow. As the handsome bridegroom has received his war orders and will ship out next week to France. New York will be emptier without him but Europe will be a safer place."

Dora didn't seem to notice that Eleanor was barely holding herself up, her hand gripping a hatstand, as she answered so quickly it didn't seem as though she had lost her composure. "Really?" said Eleanor. She faltered a little bit when she said this next bit. "What—hat is she wearing?"

Dora showed her the picture. Philip, in uniform, and a smiling Rosemary Fell in a moss-green hat that Eleanor remembered stitching. Underneath was the caption, "The soon-to-be-Mr.-and-Mrs.-Alsop".

*E*leanor feigned a headache and walked the twelve blocks to the waterfront, although she was so pale, it hadn't required a lot of acting. She stopped on the corner and bought a copy of the paper. She had always known he was betrothed, but somehow seeing it in black-and-white:

Miss Rosemary Fell and Captain Philip Alsop will be wed, a month earlier than planned . . .

She couldn't imagine that the time they'd spent together had meant nothing to him.

She saw him standing at the edge of the dock shouting orders to some shipyard workers who were loading a freighter that had just come in.

Philip smiled when he saw Eleanor approaching him. "I was hoping I would see you today," he said.

"And what about tomorrow?" she said accusingly. "Were you hoping you would see me tomorrow? And what about this?" She waved the newspaper at him. "Were you planning to tell me?"

He held her shoulders to try to calm her. She realized Rosemary Fell would never cause a scene in public. She responded flatly, almost without emotion, "What?"

He noticed that the dockworkers were staring at them and pulled Eleanor off to the side of the dock. She was beyond caring. What did she expect him to say? That he loved her. Certainly, she expected him to say that. But what declaration could he make to her? What could he promise? There wasn't anything he could say to change the way it was. There were too many feelings to account for, too much propriety at stake, too little time.

He let go of her and shut his eyes. "It's as if your life is going one way," he said finally, "and then something happens . . . Are you supposed to derail your entire life?"

She finished for him. "Or just not care about the consequences that it has on others?" He would always remember the way that she looked at him, directly, almost as if it were a challenge. "I'm a big girl," she said, "I can take care of myself."

There was a moment where neither of them spoke. "I know—" she said, "your name is supposed to appear in the papers three times—when you're born, when you marry, and when you die. And that's where I'll get my information about you."

She threw the newspaper on the ground where it landed in a puddle, opened to the offending item. The edges of the paper curled slightly as the picture of Philip and Rosemary became submerged in water. He watched her as she walked away from him down the dock.

It was late, after midnight, when Josie came in from the theater. She was elated from her performance and didn't feel like going to sleep. The light was on in Eleanor's room. She knocked softly and Eleanor, still in her street clothes, answered the door.

"Oh, it *is* there," said Josie. Eleanor forced a smile.

"Well, you are *never* here anymore. Let me in before we wake the warden." Without waiting for her to open the door fully, Josie pushed her way in.

Eleanor's bedroom was so plain, it was almost austere. Minimally decorated, a dried floral wreath with ribbons hung on the wall, and a cheap paisley shawl had been thrown over the end table as a covering. There were fresh flowers, lilies, in a vase on the table. Josie threw herself dramatically across the bed and lay on her stomach, her head propped up by her hands and elbows. "You got anything to eat? I'm starving."

"You're the one who works in a restaurant," said Eleanor.

"Not anymore. I've gotten a part. Not a part exactly. I'm part of the chorus . . ." She added, laughing, ". . . And, I'm completely broke." Eleanor tossed her an apple from the top of the bureau.

Josie was so intent on herself, she could still hear the applause from the theater, she hadn't eaten, and it took her a few moments to realize that Eleanor was not her usual self.

She noticed the necklace around her friend's neck. "Where did you get that?" asked Josie.

"I gave myself a present."

Josie wasn't buying any of it. "Some present." She took a bite of the apple. "You don't have to lie to me," she said. "He has good taste."

"I should give it back to him," she said. It was all she could do to hold back tears.

"Oh, I wouldn't do that," Josie said. "It's always a good idea to have something around you can hock in case things get tough."

Eleanor's hand flew protectively to the necklace at

this remark and it was clear, that no matter what were to occur in the future, she would never part with it.

Did she expect to hear from him, expect him to show up on her doorstep? Did she harbor any illusions that he would change his mind about the course his life was going to take? Perhaps. But she was practical enough to know that he wouldn't. And impractical enough to ever give up the notion that he would.

$\mathcal{M}$ ilitary feet marching with their own rhythm and syncopation, in contrast to the provincial French countryside they were marching through, rough, chaotic, as though it were a portent of what was to come. They received a warm reception, cheered on, fed, embraced, as if the Americans were the saviours they'd been waiting for.

As Philip wrote to Rosemary, *"It's odd. I feel as though we're on a trip. Or on a roller coaster that has started up and down is just around the corner. We stop and eat at inns along the way. Except that everyone looks frightened, awfully glad to see us though.*

"We've stopped at a small country inn for lunch. Pro-

vincial. You would like the menu. It feels so normal here as though I have a foot in my old life. The officers will sleep in beds tonight and then, I think, there will be no more inns. We are supposed to camp in Normandy.

"I want to tell you to light a candle in the window but pour a glass of wine instead. Its feeling will be more immediate."

He was sitting in the dining room of a provincial country inn as he wrote to her looking out the window at a vast expanse of rolling meadow that months later would be decimated by war. He signed his name and sealed the letter. Timothy Whitfield, a British Officer who would die two months later in a trench outside Vevey, walked over carrying a small chess set which he placed between them on the table. Philip drew white and Whitfield set the board up.

"Pawn to pawn four," said Philip. "I'm not very good at this," he mused. "I never had a head for schematics." He started to draw on the tablecloth. "It's like chess," he went on as he moved a knight out. "You have to have a head for it." He finished the sketch, perplexed. "If they come from the north and we're here . . ." He drew an arrow. He realized that he didn't know the answer.

"May the best man win . . ." said Whitfield, answering for him.

"Something like that," said Philip as he looked out

the window again at the pristine meadowland and the rows of stone houses that edged it. "But aren't I supposed to feel angry? I am angry—that you could take a history like this and trample on it."

"But, Philip," said Whitfield as he captured his knight with his pawn, "we are history."

osemary did as he asked, pouring herself a glass of burgundy because she thought it was appropriate and sat alone by the fire in the sheltered and sequestered silence of her New York parlor. The last four weeks seemed almost a blur, the chaos of the wedding where everyone around her had seemed to almost lose their minds.

Her father had turned into a child, on the morning of her wedding, forgetting how to tie his tie, presenting himself to Gertrude. "Oh, Gertrude. Are you any good at this? I've been doing it all my life and suddenly today, I can't even remember . . ."

Gertrude stifled a smile and grabbed both ends of his tie around his neck a little more forcefully than necessary. "Stand still," she told him. "I'm not going to be able to do it with you hopping around like that."

He looked at the picture of his late wife, Elizabeth, in the silver frame on the dressing room table. "I wish Elizabeth were here today, Gertrude," he said. "I need someone to hold *my* hand tonight. This is not one of those things I imagined doing alone." He looked at his perfectly tied tie in the mirror. "Thanks, Gertrude," he said and stared again at the picture of his wife. "But I think we've done well with her, Lizzie. I hope he does as well."

When Jane showed up an hour later, Rosemary's bedroom was a mess, a pre-wedding mess. The bed was unmade. There were petticoats scattered about the floor, all very frilly and girlish, and Jane felt as if she were in street clothes in the navy blue serge suit she'd picked for the wedding. Jane had declined being one of the bridesmaids. No, she would not wear a dress and attempt to catch a bouquet for an event that would never occur ... Rosemary didn't press her on it but there were a great many things in Jane's life they never spoke about. Mostly, they spoke about Rosemary. And that morning, the morning of her wedding, was no exception.

There was a breakfast tray on the vanity that appeared largely untouched. Jane helped herself to a strawberry and called out to Rose who appeared from inside the closet. She was half in her wedding gown but it wasn't fastened. Her hair was up. She looked almost pretty.

"Oh, it's you," she said sounding relieved. "I thought you were Gertrude. For twenty-seven years, every time I'm hungry, I've had to beg her to make me something. This morning, the one time I'm not hungry, she showed up with a four-course breakfast. I'm sure I've forgotten something."

"You have," said Jane. "Something borrowed. Mother sent it over." She smiled and held a black velvet jewelry box out to Rosemary.

"It's beautiful," said Rosemary as Jane fastened the emerald bracelet on her wrist.

"It's borrowed."

"I know that," said Rosemary and then added wistfully, "I wish your mother was coming."

"So do I. She hasn't been out for months. She hasn't felt well enough to go out."

"She's the only one of us, though," said Rosemary, "who never loses her mind. Philip's so nervous I think he's going to jump out of his skin. Not something I respect or admire. My father's turned into a child. And I know I can do this but I feel as if I'm giving myself a wedding. Tell me not to do this today."

Jane smiled at her. "Don't do this, today, Rose," she said. "Just be a good girl and turn around and let me fasten your dress. See how tiny your waist is. Mother says a girl's waist is supposed to be tiny before she marries. Now, look at my waist. See, I barely have one. Not that it would be my preference to marry a man." And in that moment, she acknowledged what they never spoke about. She missed a hook on Rosemary's dress. "There, hold your breath in." There was a hint of envy in her voice when she said, "You look almost like a picture."

To the outside eye, the wedding was a complete success. The day lilies practically spilled off the altar into the church. The organ played Brahms' 4th and then the Wedding March. Rosemary, protected by her veil and her exquisite bone structure, looked every bit the society bride. Her father wiped his eyes as he walked her down the aisle. The bouquet was caught by one of the Forrest girls, Nan, who went home with a piece of cake to put beneath her pillow so she might dream about who the lucky man might be.

That Teddy would tell Sarah later that Philip was a near wreck before the wedding (which he masked with charm and wit) was not surprising. But, once he'd stepped into the church, there was no evidence to anyone in the congregation of his nerves. Rosemary, distraught that their honeymoon was reduced to one night at the Plaza, was too reserved to admit to anyone that she was actually frightened it would not be enough time to properly assume her wedding vows.

A small crowd had gathered on the street. It was, after all, a society wedding, and a number of people wanted to catch a glimpse of the bride. Philip and Rosemary were practically royalty. And, in their number, far back in the crowd, was a woman whose face was partly and purposefully hidden by a veil but whose beauty was unmistakeable. Eleanor Smith. There was an innocence about her in that moment as she watched Philip kiss Rosemary at the top of the stairs. And the division between the wedding party and the people on the street was so defined, as if there were a barricade they would never be able to cross.

She watched the moment when they kissed to try to see if it measured up in any way to what they had ... She didn't wait until they walked hand-in-hand down the steps and into the waiting carriage, the back of which was decorated with bells and ribbons, but lost herself in a crowd of people and headed towards the theater where Josie was performing.

On the corner of 45th Street, there was a man, quite drunk, under a lamppost, whose age was difficult to determine. He looked to be in his sixties although he may have had ten fewer years. He was holding a bottle in his hand. He looked up and saw Eleanor and his face broke into a smile.

"I knew my little girl was going to show up today," he practically shouted.

Eleanor looked panicked. She crossed the street to avoid him, praying that he wouldn't try to follow her. She almost haphazardly fumbled in her purse, came up with a ticket and lost herself in the sea of theatergoers as they rushed inside, pretending all along that her father had mistaken her for someone else.

Inside the theater, she made her way to the bar and ordered herself a whiskey and soda, what Philip always used to order. There was a man standing at the bar staring at her. The scotch tasted vile and strangely metallic. She forced herself to finish it as though it were an homage of a sort and found her way to her seat. The performance was sold-out and she was acutely aware that she was one of the only people who had come to the theater alone. It took a long time for the curtain to rise and she couldn't quite get herself to focus on the show except for the bits when Josie bounded in.

Josie was only a part of the chorus but she had that moment, in the third act, where she performed that little song and dance with Jimmy Donohue, a large, moon-faced fellow with kind eyes and a voice that was remarkably deep. They actually stopped the show, getting their own round of applause led partly by Eleanor who certainly felt it deserved a standing ovation. It was a soppy, romantic musical and as the leads kissed, the curtain fell.

Eleanor waited with a small group of people for the actors to change their clothes. The show was a popular hit, although it had received very little critical acclaim, and there was an infectious mood among the cast. Josie was more bubbly than usual hanging on the arm of Jimmy Donohue. A man walked up who was better dressed than the rest of them, dark-haired, handsome. His name was Robert Doyle and he was the producer of the show. He couldn't take his eyes off Eleanor.

"Where have you been keeping her?" he said to Josie.

Before Josie could answer, Eleanor said, "I've just come back to town." Josie wrote it off as one of those things Eleanor said just because she liked to be mysterious, although it did occur to Josie that if Eleanor disappeared, she would have no idea, beyond the hat shop, where to look for her.

Doyle was quite taken with her, tried to talk her into coming across the street with them for a drink.

But Eleanor insisted that she wouldn't be good company that night. Doyle watched her, intrigued as she walked back through the darkened aisle of the theater alone. She took a taxi home because for one night she wanted to be just like them.

*S*omeone in the crowd began to sing "Over There." And it was picked up by one of the soldiers on the boat. There were women holding children, wiping their eyes with handkerchiefs, waving miniature American and Allied flags that had been mounted on small sticks, trying to appear brave.

It was the first deployment of U.S. troops to Europe. Three military transport ships were leaving and it seemed as if half of New York had turned out. A huge crowd had gathered on the pier. And, off to the side, a splinter group protesting the United States' involvement. There were a number of police, uniformed officers on foot and on horseback, to lend support and quiet the crowd, if need be. Rosemary had gone with Philip to the Hudson Dock to see him off. She took Jane with her so that, after he left, she wouldn't have to be alone. Rosemary was never very good in crowds. She always tried to stand a safe distance from everyone as though being part of a community interest would somehow make her common. She was not at ease with public displays of emotion, of which there were many that afternoon.

Since Philip was an officer and Rosemary behaved like she was titled gentry—they were, after all, one of those New York couples—the crowds parted to let them pass. Rosemary held on to Philip's arm tightly, as if she could never let him go. Nothing had seemed as real as this. The lobby of the Plaza had been filled, the morning after their wedding night, with soldiers—but that had seemed to Rosemary almost as if it was staged. She had been right—one night at the Plaza and best efforts not to appear petulant about it.

They had moved in with her father for Philip's remaining two nights in town. Did she intend for them to live at her father's house forever? They hadn't really had the conversation. It made sense for Rosemary to stay on 9th Street while Philip was at war but when he returned . . . shouldn't they establish their own residence, begin to have their own life, or did she expect that he would fit in neatly into hers?

She packed for him. What did you pack for someone when you were sending them to war? Stationery which she'd had engraved with just his name and no address, a quill pen, a thin volume of Yeats's "The Green Helmet and Other Poems," a bedside clock which he thought was sweet but almost comical. A wristwatch perhaps with a second hand for precise movement of military operations but that would be regulation-issue. He couldn't imagine unpacking his clock each night after he'd undone his bedroll—how like Rosemary to try to decorate his bedsite, as if there would be any vestige of civilization in a trench. He teased her that perhaps she could figure out a way to pack a bedside table.

Rosemary was standing just to the side of the gangplank as Philip walked up it to board the ship. He leaned over as he passed her. She reached her hand up to his. Their lips could not quite reach.

The crowd swelled closer to the boat, as if everyone wanted to hold on to whoever it was that was leaving them. And in their number, way in the back of the crowd, stood Eleanor Smith, partly hidden by a hat with a veil that shaded her face. She watched as Philip reached down and touched Rosemary's cheek. She wanted to touch him. She wanted to be able to kiss him goodbye. She imagined what it would be like to be "the other woman" in mourning without a recognized outlet for grief and she was reminded again of how nothing in her life had been legitimate except her feelings for Philip.

Say a prayer.

The departing soldiers continued to sing. They were joined by the people in the crowd.

Neither Philip nor Rosemary sang. The only expression on Philip's face was to blink quickly as he looked down at Rosemary. Jane caught Rose's arm and held it.

The crowd continued singing. As Rosemary and Jane watched Philip walk up to the deck and in that moment become indistinguishable from the other soldiers in uniform, Rosemary turned and looked at Jane. "I never have the right response anymore," she said. "I don't want to wave a flag. I'll wave a flag when he comes home."

Jane held Rose's arm a little tighter as the ship began to pull away.

*O*nce abroad, entrapped in a regimen he barely understood, where
everything was minimal and stripped away and basic
and terrifying, and though he could admit this to no
one, plagued with lingering doubts about his ability to
lead and the nature of war, images of Eleanor kept
coming to his mind. He sent her a letter from France.
A letter she read so many times that the paper had
grown thin in the places where she held it.

She was sitting on a stool in the workroom re-
reading the letter, although she had no need since she
knew it by heart, when Dora walked into the work-

room carrying a black hat. She immediately hid the letter in the pocket of her apron.

Dora held the hat out to her. "Would you mind . . . ? We have a delivery to make. Mrs. Lawson—her husband," said Dora as if no other explanation were necessary. "I've grown to hate this war. But my mother always used to say, one should always be prepared and keep a black hat in the closet."

Eleanor couldn't tell whether she'd just been told a life lesson or one of Dora's eccentricities. She took the hat from Dora gingerly and put it in a hat box. Forgetting that the letter was in the pocket, she took her apron off and hung it on a hook. She nodded as Dora handed her the address.

"Although," said Dora as Eleanor turned to go, "I guess I could understand wanting a new hat under the circumstances."

It was terribly hot and humid. A group of children were playing around an open fire hydrant, barefoot, unmindful of the fact that their clothes were getting wet. Three women, presumably with some relation to the children, sat exhausted, legs splayed, fanning themselves on a stoop. Eleanor walked by carrying the hat box. She felt like a messenger of death. And as she walked down the street, the words in Philip's letter, the letter she'd been reading, the letter she hadn't expected to get and hoped for every day, sounded over in her mind.

"I have heard of people having flashbacks when they returned from war," he wrote. *"But I began to have them as soon as I arrived. Flashbacks of you. They come unbidden. I'm hoping you can forgive me and give me a chance to make right what is wrong. In the meantime, I am left with memories of you. The way you looked when you opened your door at night . . . And how it felt to lie beside you . . ."*

A taxi honked at Eleanor as she crossed the street. She hurried on oblivious. The sounds of the city became intermingled with the sound of war in her imagination, an explosion in the distance, planes flying overhead.

"Did I speak to you about duty. I meant to . . ."

Eleanor walked down a residential street that was lined with brownstones with a uniform facade.

"Duty and honor. And what it is like to be bound to one thing when your heart wishes you to do something else . . ."

The sound of a bomber overhead, intermixed with traffic noise as it strafes the sky.

"What it is like to fight a war when nothing about a war makes sense except a sense of duty."

The sound of a single bomb now on a swift trajectory to the ground as if for one moment she were by his side.

"Don't question my love. Try, if you can to forgive me. And know that I am coming home to you."

And then, unmistakably, the sound of a bomb as it hit and exploded on the ground.

The Lawson house stood out because of the yellow ribbon on the door that was tied like a Christmas package, but in the center where the bow would be, hung a black wreath. Eleanor walked down the stairs of the brownstone to the servants' and delivery entrance and knocked.

The door was opened by the fat cook, Emma, whose normally cheerful countenance was stained by tears. The sight of the hat box was enough to start her off again, but she had always run a gracious household. "You must be scorched," she said to Eleanor. "I've got fresh lemonade."

Eleanor was feeling flushed and queasy from the heat. She held the banister to steady herself.

"Come in out of the sun," said Emma. "Not that it's much better in here. What with the baking for tomorrow."

"Have you a—" Eleanor was going to ask for a Powder Room but she was too polite.

Emma guessed her meaning. "You do look as though you might be sick," she said and directed

Eleanor to follow her through the kitchen to the servants' bath. Emma, protective of the house from strangers, waited outside the door and heard the unmistakable sound of retching even though Eleanor had turned the water on to mask it.

A moment later, Eleanor opened the door. She had splashed water on her face and her color had returned a bit. The two women looked at each other. "It's the heat," said Eleanor apologetically.

"If I were you," said Emma who guessed her condition immediately, "I would loosen those stays." Eleanor seemed to pale at this suggestion. She followed the woman back to the kitchen. "I suppose I should see if it fits—see if the hat fits," said Eleanor.

"Oh, no—" said the old cook, handing her a glass of lemonade. "I'll take it up to her. I don't think either one of you's up to a fitting." They both looked for a moment at the hat box on the table.

When Josie came in at her usual time, twelve-thirty, from the theater, carrying a chilled bottle of champagne, she found Eleanor sitting at the vanity in her room wearing only white pantalooned underwear. The window was open and the overhead fan was spinning slowly, but all it seemed to do was move the hot and humid air from one place to another.

"You missed my applause," said Josie reproachfully.

Eleanor had promised to meet her at the theater that night but hadn't felt well enough.

"I brought the house down," said Josie. "It was fabulous." She practically pirouetted around the room and popped the cork on the champagne. She poured them each a glass in jam jars which was the only readily available china she could find.

"Where were you?" she asked as she handed Eleanor a glass.

"I wasn't feeling well. It was the heat. I haven't been—feeling well. Dora sent me on a delivery, at noon. I thought I'd walk. It was too far to walk in the heat. Someone's husband died and I—had to bring them a black hat. It—it was too far to walk in the heat."

"You look pale," said Josie.

"I do look pale. I know," said Eleanor. "I shouldn't. I should look like a picture of health. I'm—" Eleanor studied her friend. It wasn't that she was worried what Josie would think of her. Josie had always dealt in unconditional acceptance. It was just that she had not yet said it out loud. "I'm—having a baby."

"You're not . . . ?!" said Josie.

"I am."

"Who is he?" asked Josie sounding in that moment like an older sister.

She didn't know how to answer. The man she loved. The father of her child. "He isn't here," she said. "He isn't—free. He's in . . . France."

"Oh great," said Josie without losing a beat. "A married soldier."

"Officer," said Eleanor.

"That makes it better," said Josie. "Have you thought about what you're going to do?! What happens when you lose your job?! How long can you hide it?!"

"I figured you'd have your name on the marquee by then and support us both," said Eleanor who was only half kidding.

"Be serious," said Josie. "I have a friend who knows a doctor. Actually, I think he's a dentist."

Eleanor cut her off. "I could never do that."

"What are you going to do then? You think Wetzel will let you live here?"

"We'll move. You've always wanted an apartment. I haven't," she said. "I haven't thought about any of it." She laughed a little to herself. "It's not a condition you think your way into. I've thought about what I will name her," she said. "If it's a girl, I want to call her Tess."

Josie answered drily, "And if it's a boy?"

"I thought I would let his father name him." Eleanor got up and walked to the window. "It would be easy to say the war has made us do things we otherwise wouldn't have."

"Us?" said Josie.

"Okay, me, then," Eleanor admitted. "But I don't have the sense to regret any of it at all." She gave an odd smile because she didn't regret any of the time she'd spent with Philip.

Would she have been more careful with Philip's letter if she had known that there would be no others? Did she leave it behind on purpose because she wanted to be discovered or had she simply become forgetful and skittish as so many women do in the early months of pregnancy?

Dora found it in the pocket of the work apron. She didn't hesitate for a moment about reading it. Eleanor was so mysterious, didn't ramble on at the drop of a hat, as did most of the girls Dora had hired and reveal the most intimate details of their lives whether Dora was interested or not. No, Eleanor had secrets. Yet, even so, Dora was surprised, not so much by the contents of the letter but by the name of its sender. Philip Alsop. Eleanor and Philip Alsop. Dora folded the letter carefully in its envelope, put it in her purse, left the shop, and locked the door behind her even though it was the middle of the afternoon.

Jane didn't hear her come in. The first thing she was aware of was Dora's arm around her waist and then Dora was kissing her neck lightly. Jane's mother was upstairs and physically unable to navigate the steps alone, so Jane felt free to let her hand rest on Dora's thigh. But that was not the intention of Dora's visit.

Dora put the letter in front of Jane on the desk and stood behind her while she read it. Dora was of the mind that they should tell Rosemary about it immediately but Jane stopped her. She took the letter from Dora and put it in the desk drawer. She locked the drawer and put the key in her pocket as if that would somehow keep the secret safe.

Jane couldn't see the point of revealing it to Rosemary (Jane's part in it aside), why did she need to know? Philip was at war and if he never returned . . . why did she need to have knowledge of his betrayal?

Dora, on the other hand, was convinced that Eleanor had behaved improperly and swore that she was going to give her notice.

Jane took some issue with that. Philip had behaved improperly. Why did Eleanor get blamed? They had a bit of a fight over this. And in the three years since they had been lovers, they'd never fought. But the definition of an affair, which is surely what Eleanor and Philip were having, is that it involves and affects more than two people which is how it comes by its name.

They shouldn't have wasted any time arguing about Eleanor's fate for, as it turned out, the girl had devised her own plan. When Dora returned to the hat shop, Eleanor was waiting for her.

After Mrs. Witherspoon had been fitted with a new hat for church and been sent out into the street with the hat already on her head, Eleanor said to Dora, "I was hoping I might speak to you."

"That's curious," said Dora, "I was wanting to speak to you, too."

Eleanor took the liberty of sitting across from her at the desk instead of standing, as she usually did, a discreet distance away. "I've been very happy here," she said. "And I appreciate the opportunity you've given me. I'm not really suited to working in a store."

Dora, who was poised to give her notice, was astonished.

Eleanor went on . . . "The people, you know," and it began to sound a bit as if it were a prepared speech, practiced and refined for its effect. "It takes a certain personality," she said. "You have it. I am too moody. Too flighty. I've learned an enormous amount from you." Her manner was both polite and oddly menacing. "Some of your customers like me. I think, is it not true, that sales have gone up since I have been here? I would like it if you would let me design for you." She looked at Dora directly. "You have customers who like my work. I wouldn't like to take business away from you." She said this last bit softly but the threat was implicit.

Dora agreed immediately. "Of course, you wouldn't," she said as she'd considered the possibilities and realized she didn't want to lose part of her clientele in the middle of a war. "There would be a lot of details to work out," said Dora.

"Whatever you think is fair," said Eleanor who instinctively knew that in business, as in life, there was never a need to press after you'd won. And though Dora concealed it from Jane for some time, it seemed she wouldn't be completely gone from their lives then.

As shabby as Wetzel's Boarding House was, it had afforded Josie and Eleanor each a certain respectability. It wasn't quite proper at the time for two women to live in an apartment alone, but they rented an apartment and concocted a story that made them look more respectable than they really were.

They claimed that Eleanor was married, for, of course, she would need to be married—she was so thin, the baby had started to show immediately—to Josie's brother, "Frank", who was properly at war which wasn't far from the truth except that Josie didn't have a brother. Josie bought a thin platinum band from

Dentons' and made Eleanor wear it on her ring finger. When Eleanor tried to pay her for it, Josie insisted that since Eleanor was married to her "brother," it was only fitting Josie should buy the ring. They sort of enjoyed the story as it gave them a public way to be protective of each other.

Joe the doorman would say to Josie tipping his hat as she walked in carrying a bag of groceries, "Afternoon, Miss Kennedy. How's your sister doing today?"

"She's fine, Joe, thanks," Josie said smiling which wasn't really the truth.

Eleanor never left the apartment. Josie did the shopping and delivered the hats for her to Dora's taking a certain pleasure in flouncing into the hat shop looking as bohemian and actressy as possible. It was all Dora could do to get her out the door as quickly as possible. She kept cash on hand, sealed in an envelope, because Josie made her plainly uncomfortable.

Eleanor would sit in the chair in the living room by the window most of the day sewing hats, occasionally reading or leafing through magazines and studying the fashions. She was so pregnant that the only way she could stitch was to balance the hat on her stomach. "I wish I could go out on the street for a walk," she said mournfully.

Josie offered to go with her but Eleanor declined. "I hardly know four people in this part of the city," she said, "but I'm sure the second I go out, I'll run into one of them. Do you think our mail's being forwarded from Wetzel's?" That was what she was really upset about, that she hadn't heard from Philip.

"I'm sure it is," said Josie. "I got some today."

"I haven't had a letter from him for a month."

Josie didn't say anything.

"Oh you think he's just forgotten me?"

"I didn't say that," said Josie. "It must be—it must be hard to send mail. The paper says they're on the move."

"The paper that you keep hiding from me," said Eleanor accusingly. "The paper that says that there are heavy casualties . . ."

"In the North," said Josie trying to calm her. "I didn't think that he was in the North. I think that you should eat something."

"I don't want to eat anything." She made a face and pushed herself out of the chair. "I'll make you a sandwich, Josie. You've got a show tonight." She hesitated in the doorway of the kitchen. "It's the waiting that's hard," she said. "And not knowing whether you're waiting for anything at all. You think that I'm a fool for waiting."

Josie shook her head because she knew that nothing she could say would change Eleanor's mind.

Eleanor had always figured the angles, but when

she figured the angles here, they didn't add up. Her mother used to tell her, "Don't fall in love, Leni. When you fall in love, you lose your sense." This was what it was then. She'd fallen in love. And she knew in her heart, even though the odds weren't in her favor, there wasn't anything else worth waiting for.

It was a Catholic Hospital. St. Mary's. There was a large wooden cross on the wall behind Eleanor's bed. All of the nurses wore nuns' habits and, she imagined, would be fairly unforgiving if they knew her true circumstances—but it was the middle of a war and no one thought that it was odd that the baby's father wasn't at her side.

Her labor was quick and forgotten as soon as they put the baby in her arms. She was beautiful, perfectly formed, long legs and feet that arched like a ballerina's, milk-white skin and little wisps of brown hair that Eleanor thought felt like silk.

"I will never let you know the things that I know," she promised, the first time she took her to her breast. "I will never let you be cold or hungry or frightened in the middle of the night."

She named her Tess. The last name was more of an issue. "Kennedy," Josie insisted. "You have to make it all seem aboveboard." It was an overt fabrication to put on the baby's birth certificate: Father: Frank Kennedy. But she had no right to use the name Alsop. And it was, Josie convinced her, a necessary lie.

Josie and Jimmy Donohue rented a carriage for the morning so they could take the baby home in style. Josie had never seen Eleanor happier, unaware as they were that as their carriage passed Fifth Avenue a military car with two soldiers in the back was on its way to Rosemary's house.

𝓜r. Fell was in his study cataloguing butterflies. He was placing a particularly large blue monarch under glass when the doorbell rang. He ignored it and continued with his work but then it rang again.

"Why isn't anyone getting the door?" he muttered under his breath. And then got up to answer the door himself.

There were two young soldiers on the doorstep. They looked grave and somber. One of them was holding a telegram in his hand. Mr. Fell knew instantly why they had come but he was silent and let them speak. "We are looking for Mrs. Philip Alsop," said the younger of the two.

"Could I suggest that you go away so that none of us will know of this?" said Mr. Fell. "No, I guess I could not suggest that." Not that it would have done any good as Rosemary's car pulled up at the curb as he added, sadly, "Yes, I imagined that you were."

Rosemary had been to lunch at "21" with Jane where the disproportionate number of women in the room and the fact that it was a meatless day emphasized the presence of the war. They had taken a walk down Fifth Avenue, Rosemary's driver following in the car a discreet distance behind, so he would be waiting at the curb as soon as they were ready to go home. After a few forays into stores, they piled safely into the backseat of the car with their packages and drove downtown. They pulled up in front of the house as the two soldiers were still standing on the doorstep. Rosemary turned absolutely white and gripped Jane's arm.

The soldiers knew no details, only that Philip had been reported dead. They had found his dog tag on a battlefield but, as yet, had been unable to identify a body. Rosemary's face hardened into a porcelain mask. If there was no physical evidence, there was no way they could know for sure. Maybe he'd . . . there were so many possibilities. She fastened onto the phrase, ". . . unable to identify the body."

When someone dies, time seems to take on a dimension of its own. Minutes expand to sometimes seem like hours and silence is filled with memories of what has been. It was not a traditional mourning period, however, as Rosemary refused to acknowledge it.

Jane went with her to Carlysle's funeral home on Madison Avenue. The floors were thickly carpeted and they noticed everybody seemed to speak in whispers. A white-faced fellow led them into Oliver Carlysle's office and left them alone. The furniture was leather. Carlysle's desk top was bare except for a conservative floral arrangement, white chrysanthemums and baby's breath, which somehow made its own statement. Rosemary and Jane, each clad in appropriately dark clothes and Rosemary wearing a black hat with a wide brim. She kept her head bowed so that it was difficult to see her eyes. She seemed nervous.

"I don't know how you have a funeral without a body," she said to Jane. "I guess we could just bury the telegram."

Jane was stunned and didn't know if she was supposed to laugh. But before she could respond, Oliver

Carlysle, the proprietor of the funeral home, entered. He looked as one would have expected him to look, so pale as to appear pasty with slightly pudgy, well-manicured hands. He mistakenly extended his hand to Jane, who realized that she didn't want to take it. "Mrs. Alsop—" he said.

Rosemary stood. "*I* am Mrs. Alsop."

"Would you forgive me?" Carlysle said immediately. "I would like to express our condolences," he said using a peculiar third-person liberty that made Jane wonder whether he imagined he was speaking on behalf of the entire spirit world.

Rosemary cut him off. "Yes, of course," she said.

He took a large book out of his desk drawer and placed it on the desk top. "There are a great many decisions to make at a time like this," he said. "We have a great many resting grounds and caskets to choose from . . ."

He turned the book towards her and in it were various pictures, drawn in gray and brown charcoal, of coffins, mahogany, pine, some elaborately carved, and headstones made of marble, granite, and simple stone. There was something so austere about them, dark, lonely, somber.

"Would you forgive *me*?" said Rosemary, standing. "I can't go through with this." She turned and walked out of the office as a fairly startled Mr. Carlysle stared after her. Jane didn't know what she was supposed to do, it wasn't her place to make the arrangements. She smiled apologetically and left the room leaving Mr. Carlysle alone with his white chrysanthemums.

The thought of it sitting empty with a headstone. Somber. Lonely. Not a place she could ever visit . . .

Jane caught up with her on Madison Avenue although as she watched her walk up the avenue, she considered it might be good for Rose to have some time alone.

"Rose, wait!" she called out. "We'll find somewhere else."

"I don't want to find somewhere else," said Rosemary as she stopped in front of a clothing shop. There was a female mannequin in the window dressed in a brown suit with a long skirt and well-tailored jacket.

"Well, what *are* you going to do?" Jane asked her.

"Not have a funeral," she answered as if it were all as simple as that. "Not have a funeral until there's a body. Until there's a body, we can't be certain."

"But," Jane said softly, "they said there was no doubt. That the firefight was so extensive there was— nothing left."

"But I'm not certain," said Rosemary. She looked at the suit in the window of the shop. "Do you like that suit?" she asked Jane.

"It's all right," said Jane, startled she was being asked to comment on a piece of clothing. "It looks like it might be difficult to walk in."

"It's not quite mourning," said Rosemary. "But then again, I don't want to be in mourning."

Rosemary opened the door of the shop and walked in. She couldn't imagine bringing flowers to an empty grave. Jane followed her into the shop having decided it was better to pretend it was an ordinary afternoon.

To the outside eye, Rosemary's life remained much the same as always except she became more civic-minded, took on more charity work and volunteered at the V.A. Hospital which seemed out of character to Jane since Rose couldn't stand the sight of blood. "I don't actually do nursing," she said to Jane when she queried her. "I read to them, talk to them. If Philip were— I wish I could do more." She was halfway convinced that Philip was lying in a hospital somewhere, a victim of amnesia. Jane thought she'd read too many books.

Jane couldn't actually say anything to Rosemary

about any of this, not that it had been easy to offer varying opinions before. She was firm in the belief that if something had happened to Philip, she would know it and until such time, she would simply operate as if he were coming home.

She refused to allow the papers to run a death notice, trading on family connections, she convinced the editor at the *Times* to make no notice of it.

Her father was worried about her, in a way that went beyond parental concern. He realized he would have felt better if she'd screamed, yelled, taken to her bed, evidenced some of the frailer and more hysterical traits of her gender. He wondered how he'd raised a child who was so implacable and didn't trust it. He suggested that they take a trip to Cape Cod to his sister's, maybe by the seaside she would rest, maybe she would finally cry, but Rosemary refused. "No, Papa," she said. "We can't do it now. We have too many obligations here. Besides, if we were to get word of him . . . If you feel the need, Papa, to visit with your sister, go on ahead, by all means."

"No," said her father, "it's your choice. And I'd rather stay with you here."

He wondered if he should have forced the issue. The flowers that were sent as condolences, Rosemary refused to accept and had them all sent on to the Veterans' Hospital. "It will surely cheer them up," she said. And no one was allowed to visit unless they had two or three amusing stories to tell. Rosemary would not discuss the war. And life on 9th Street went on much the way it had, as though there had never been a telegram.

It occurred to Jane shortly after the telegram arrived that Eleanor Smith would have no way of knowing about Philip, given the press black-out, and she felt it was her responsibility to bear the news. It took some prodding to get the address out of Dora who, finally, confessed to Jane that she had kept her on.

"I went to give her notice. And she gave me notice instead." Dora laughed nervously. "I was afraid that— She suggested that she should design for me. And that my customers like her work. They do, you know. If I hadn't," she said, "she would have gone to Ella's

Haberdashery or some-such . . ." Dora was frightened Jane would be angry with her.

"You don't have to explain to me," said Jane.

"Don't I?" said Dora. "I feel responsible. They met in my shop, you know."

"No," said Jane, "they met before. They met the same day I met her. I sent her to you. Remember?"

"Yes," said Dora. "I'd forgotten that."

"Have you seen her?" asked Jane.

"Never comes in herself," said Dora with a bit of an edge. "Has her actress girlfriend bring the hats in," she said. Her opinion of Eleanor had been colored by her business dealings with her. She didn't guess the real reason for it and that Eleanor's condition had made her unable to show herself. "Quite the little star, our Eleanor," she said. "But she's talented. She designed this." She held up a beige hat with very simple lines. "I think it would look good on you."

Jane tried it on. "I'll take it," she said and insisted on paying for it, "as long as you give me her address."

There was no answer at the apartment but as Jane was leaving the building, she ran into Eleanor entering the lobby pushing Tess in her carriage.

One look at the child's face made Jane certain of whose child she was.

"My roommate's baby," Eleanor said much too quickly. And then added, "Were you looking for me?" with that curious open quality she had that could be so disarming.

Jane hadn't been expecting the baby and suddenly couldn't bring herself to tell Eleanor about Philip's death. "I was," she said. "But I'll stop back. It's—late. I'll stop back another time."

"The hat looks good on you," said Eleanor. She hesitated. "I would have given you one."

She wanted to ask her about Philip. It had been six months since she'd heard from him. But how could she ask about Philip . . .

"She's pretty," said Jane, looking at the baby.

"Yes, she is," said Eleanor. "And even tempered. I'm glad you like the hat," she said again.

"Yes, it's my style," said Jane. "Plain. Usually. Plain and direct. Not always."

Eleanor was quite agitated when she got upstairs to her apartment. She was convinced that Jane had come to tell her something. It seemed so odd she'd had no letter from him. She put Tess down for a nap, then changed her mind and bundled the child in warm clothes, put a blanket over her in the stroller, and walked the many blocks to the Armory, almost as if it were a vigil.

There was a list of dead and missing, handwritten, posted on the outside gate. Philip's name wasn't on it. She pushed her way into the War Office past the line of waiting women with children hanging on their skirts.

The building was institutional like a bad school, the walls may have started out yellow or green but had aged to be a hybrid contributing to the grim, efficient, oddly oppressive atmosphere. Eleanor was aware of the sound her shoes made as she walked to the end of the hall to an office marked by a plaque which said, "Office of War Information." She spoke to a middle-aged secretary in military dress.

She took a seat on the wooden bench holding the blanketed, sleeping Tess against her shoulder as the secretary went to inquire if General Armstrong would see her.

"He'll see you," said the woman. "I thought he would."

Eleanor walked into the General's Office and took a seat across from him. Tess was sleeping in her arms.

"I've come—to ask about my—brother," she said.

How many conversations like this had he had in the past few months. "His name, please," said the General in low and measured tones.

"Captain Philip Alsop."

He hesitated. He knew what had happened to Philip Alsop. He shifted some papers on his desk. He looked curiously at Eleanor. He didn't remember that Alsop had a sister.

"The casualties have been so extensive," he said. "There isn't a family in New York that hasn't been touched by this." He didn't need to say more. There was no doubt about what came after that sentence, although he went on in some detail.

The next thing Eleanor was aware of, she was on the street, as though she'd lost a patch of time, had no memory of anything except staring at the map of Europe on the wall behind the desk strategically marked with thumbtacks . . . and then she was pushing the baby down Lexington, gripping the handles of the stroller so tightly, her knuckles were whitened, lost in a memory of her own.

The carriage pulled up on a street corner that looked more like an alleyway. There was laundry hanging from windows and people standing idly on street corners as if they had nowhere else to go. The carriage stopped in front of a tenement building. An old woman was evident in an upstairs window hanging sheets on a rope of clothesline.

A twelve-year-old girl with a dirty face and a torn dress sat on the stoop of a building next door. Her shoes looked as if the soles were worn, cold, sitting there without a sweater.

Eleanor turned to Philip in the carriage next to her. "You wanted to see where I'm from," she said. "A street just like this one. A street you'd find in any city, if you chose to look for it."

She pulled the silk shawl tighter around her shoulders.

Philip spoke to the driver. "We can go now," he said.

Did she imagine in that moment that he was taking her away from it forever?

When she got back to the apartment, she put Tess down in her crib.

He will never see his baby.

She walked over and looked at herself in the mirror.

Slowly, she undid the many buttons of her dress. She put a hand on her breast and tried to lose herself in a memory of her own. In the crib, Tess started crying. She walked over and gently rocked the crib and began to sing to her.

Hush little baby, don't say a word.
Papa's going to buy you a mockingbird.
And if that mockingbird don't sing . . .

Her voice cracked.

There was a mobile hanging over the baby's crib, glass petals in the shape of teardrops that in the day-time caught the light and splashed a rainbow across the quilt. She knocked the mobile and the petals made a sound like bells.

When Josie came home with Jimmy Donohue, Eleanor was asleep in the chair in the living room wrapped in the silk shawl. She woke up as soon as she heard the front door shut. Her face was streaked from crying.

"He's dead, Josie. He's dead. And he's never com-ing back to me." She began to cry uncontrollably. Josie slipped herself into the chair beside her friend and held her head in her lap until she'd quieted down. In the next room, the baby started to cry and Jimmy Donohue went to comfort her. "It's no different than it was," said Eleanor looking up at Josie. "I always knew I'd be alone with her."

And then she said no more about it. She didn't go out for a week. Josie and Jimmy Donohue took care of her and Tess.

It was shortly after this that she took up with the producer, Robert Doyle, who, understanding the circumstances of her life, treated her as if she were a rare and fragile creature.

Doyle was content to wait and in the meantime take whatever she felt that she could offer. He liked having her on his arm. He formed a strong attachment to the baby whom he showered with gifts. No one understood why she didn't marry Doyle; a lot of girls in her situation would have. Except she once said to Josie, by way of explanation, "I can't do it unless I feel that I can love him." Outwardly, Eleanor seemed to be all right, but she was so much about looking one way when she actually felt another, that it was difficult to tell. She and Rosemary had that in common.

As for Jane Howard, she felt as if she were observing a situation where everyone around her, partly due to their lack of information and skewed perceptions, was in an altered state. A situation she could correct if she set her mind to it, if she could only see her way clear to do that. She unburdened herself one night to her mother, whose counsel she hadn't sought since she was ten. "What would you do," Jane asked her, "if you knew that Christina's husband was having an affair?"

"My Christina?" Her mother laughed. "It wouldn't be the first time." Jane Howard's mother was raised in Vienna and, as a result, freer about these things than many of the other women in New York although Jane had never felt at liberty to discuss her own preferences with her mother. Jane always imagined she suspected though since she'd never given her one of those lectures. "When are you going to get married, dear?" She never asked Jane why she didn't seem interested in suitors.

"No," said Jane, "I meant, what would I do if I knew that my best friend's husband was having an affair . . . ?"

"*Your* best friend," said Malina. "But I thought Philip was—"

"Reported dead," said Jane. "He was. But he was having an affair and the woman he was having an affair with had a baby."

"Are you certain it was his baby?"

"Fairly certain."

"I would do nothing. I don't see what this has to do with you."

"Because I intruded," said Jane. And, after a moment, it all came rushing out, in some detail, the story of the first night Rosemary had happened on Eleanor, picked her up, so to speak, and then unceremoniously booted her into the street, how Jane had followed her after Rose had tossed her out and given her the address of Dora's Hat Shop. She tried to explain how she felt she was complicitous when Philip started seeing

Eleanor, how she had egged him on, delighted in it, unmindful of the consequences all of it might have.

"If I'd just let her continue walking down the street," Jane said, "if I hadn't encouraged him . . ."

"But you're not responsible," her mother said.

"I feel responsible," said Jane. She laughed. "And slightly incompetent. When I went to tell Eleanor about Philip and saw the baby, I couldn't tell her anything at all. And now," she said nervously, "I feel that I ought to tell Rosemary—it's the child that changes it—but I don't know how to tell Rose. I'm a sorry excuse for a go-between."

"That's not a terrible thing," said Jane's mother, "a go-between is just a step up from a gigolo."

"Then, that is what I am," said Jane, "because I think Rosemary has a right to know."

It was with some determination that Jane showed up, a few hours later, at Rosemary's door. She noticed the house was strangely lit from inside, as though it were faintly glowing. She rang the bell and, after a moment, Rosemary answered it.

"Jane!" she gushed at her, "This is a surprise! We were just—I would've invited you . . ." She looked embarrassed. "But it didn't seem like your style. But I'm so awfully glad you're here." She whispered in Jane's ear. "You've heard about this woman. Madame Olga? Everybody's seeing her. We're—having a séance." She hustled Jane inside. "Take off your coat and gloves. We all have to touch hands." She giggled. "Can I get you a drink?" And then she got oddly serious and this next bit she said was quite strange. "You see I want her to try to contact Philip, because if she can't . . ." her voice trailed off but her meaning was clear.

She poured Jane a glass of champagne and pulled her into the drawing room which was lit, as was the rest of the house, only by candles which accounted for the strange, ethereal glow outside. Madame Olga was seated at the head of a card table that had been set up for the occasion. She was in her late forties, with the kind of skin that had seen too much sun, she had a silk scarf wrapped around her head and very large earrings, the stones of which appeared to be black opals. Her hair fell out from the scarf in curly wisps about her face. Her eyes were green and quite compelling. And it was clear she had a bit of a temper if pushed. Her accent appeared to be Rumanian.

Rosemary set her glass of champagne on the table and pulled a chair up for Jane. "Jane Howard," she said, "I would like you to meet"—she gestured dramatically—"Madame Olga. Psychic seer extraordinaire." Madame Olga nodded her turbanned head. Jane nodded back in somewhat identical if mocking fashion.

"You know everyone else," said Rosemary, as seated at the table were Teddy and Sarah Porterville and Rosemary's father.

"Do not ask," said Rosemary's father, "how I was talked into this."

Jane laughed and took a seat next to him. "I won't," she said.

Jane said hello to the other people seated there as Rosemary took her place next to Madame Olga.

The room was absolutely still. The candles flickered. The air seemed thick as though it were ripe for visions, although Jane suspected it was because the doors and windows were shut, the furnace was on, and there was a healthy fire burning in the fireplace.

Madame Olga threw her head back for effect, then put her hands out to touch her fingers to Rosemary on one side and Teddy Porterville on the other. She looked at them all for a moment, then bowed her head. The rest of them did the same, reaching their hands out to touch the fingers of the people on either side.

When Madame Olga spoke it was with a heavy accent. Her voice was deep and guttural. "The spirits are here," she said, "if only we can reach them . . . I want everyone to touch their fingers to the fingers of the person next to them. Feel . . ." She said the word "feel" as though it had more than one syllable in it.

"...the energy from your spirit fusing with theirs..."

Rosemary whispered to Jane across the table. "It's a test you see to see if she can summon Philip... but so far she hasn't been able to do it..."

"Silence," said Madame Olga forcefully. "I need quiet, madame, so they can break through to our space and time..."

Madame Olga swooned her head back. "The spirits are here," she said, "if only we can reach them. I feel that they are near us. I sense that they are near us. There is something here."

The chandelier above the table began to sway slightly, the candles dimmed as if they were about to go out. Jane tried to assess if there was a trick here, if the chandelier had been rigged by wires. The room felt suddenly cold.

"They are around us..." said Madame Olga. And then her trance-like swoon was broken as the doorbell rang.

"I'll get it," said Rosemary jumping up from her seat.

Madame Olga began to mutter something under her breath in gypsy to the effect of "Fucking debutantes, they do not understand the sacredness of the moment." But everyone in the room just thought this was part of her gypsy spirit chant.

Rosemary walked to the front door and opened it. There was a man standing on the steps in a regulation issue army coat. He was so thin and strangely taller than she had remembered him.

There was a soldier in an army vehicle parked at the curb. *Was it possible . . . ?*

"I seem to have misplaced my key," he said.

"Philip . . . ?" And then she was in his arms, alternately kissing his face and resting her head on his shoulder, holding onto him as though she would never let him go. "Philip! Oh, my darling, you're home."

She swept back into the drawing room hanging onto Philip's arm. She was smiling for the first time in months.

"Madame Olga," she said, "you're fabulous! I will recommend you to all my friends."

And then she turned to Jane. "Jane! Jane! Philip's home." But Jane had already jumped up from her seat to throw her arms around him.

*D*id they notice right away that something was wrong with him? He was distant. They thought he was fatigued, worn down, shell-shocked. God knew what he'd been through. They were never able to get him to talk about it much.

They discussed it the first night. Jane said, in her usually direct fashion, "You were a prisoner?"

"I was an officer," Philip said as though he had disdain for his own position. "I was treated better than a prisoner."

They all felt as if the answers they received had been rehearsed, as if he'd been through a debriefing and had been coached on what he was allowed to tell . . . and that there was a subtext to it all. That he felt in some way he had had more to do with the enemy than he would have liked.

Teddy tried to make light of it. He joked, "But there was barbed wire and all that stuff, right? Torture?"

Philip denied this.

"Come on—did they put you in isolation?"

Philip shook his head.

The only one of them who seemed to have any real understanding of it was Rosemary's father. "There's a syndrome," he said, "where a prisoner starts to identify with his captors . . ."

Philip added, "Or associate with them and feels a certain amount of guilt about that."

Sarah Porterville piped in, "I have an uncle who avoided capture by taking refuge in a brothel."

"For a night?" asked Teddy.

"No, three months," said Sarah. "My aunt had a terrible time with him when he came home . . ."

Everyone laughed except Philip who finished the brandy in his glass and poured himself another. "There were no brothels," he said, "but the Germans had a lot of willing women."

"It doesn't matter," said Rosemary. "It doesn't matter what it was—you're home now."

By the old Moulmein Pagoda,
lookin' eastward to the sea . . .

It was Rosemary's father's favorite poem, Kipling's "Mandalay" and, as he read it aloud to himself, it sounded almost melodic. They'd had a quiet dinner at home, Mr. Fell and Rosemary and Philip without outside interference. A rack of lamb, quince jelly, potatoes that had been roasted in their skins, and a twelve-year old St. Emilion that Mr. Fell had carefully selected from the wine cellar. Rosemary was bubbly, vivacious, seeming to almost flutter about the room, not letting Philip or her father assist in any of the serving and jumping up, much to Gertrude's shock, to help clear the dishes.

After dinner, they'd retired to the living room and

had a long, spirited discussion about Braque. At eleven, Philip was tired and Rosemary went up to bed with him.

As they climbed the stairs, they heard Mr. Fell reading to himself from Kipling's "Mandalay."

By the old Moulmein Pagoda,
lookin' eastward to the sea,
There's a Burma girl a-settin'
an' I know she thinks o' me:
For the wind is in the palm-trees
an' the temple bells they say:
"Come you back, you British soldier;
come you back to Mandalay!"

Rosemary smiled but the soft, hushed way he was reading made it sound almost like a prayer.

Upstairs, Rosemary shut the door to their bedroom. She turned to Philip. She seemed playful in a grown-up kind of way. She slowly undid the buttons of her dress to her waist. She was, in that moment, completely open, uninhibited. She smiled and walked towards him. She put his hand on her breast and then he buried his face there. He began to kiss her . . . She would show him that she could be more than a society wife, that she was capable of real passion, that all the months of waiting for him had built into a longing, a pining that she could no longer contain. Kiss me there, Philip. She felt chills, a tremor of excitement that tingled down her spine.

And then his passion changed to something else and he broke down. She comforted him as best she could. She was thrown, her reactions were off, she was hurt. If she'd had the sense to talk to him about it or rather let him speak to her about what it was like to be out in the raw night with the stars overhead as they always were, curious, the placement of the stars never changed just shifted in the sky in relation to each other as the year marched on, cold, wet in the muddy trench, afraid to move, terrified that at any moment there would be a flash of light or the shrill aching sound of a shell as it pierced the air. Keep a stiff upper lip, a cool facade, your head about you. Can't let the men know that you're afraid. Keep a cool surface. Calm. Detached. As inside a part of you has been shattered.

he sun streamed in through the windows in filtered lines. There was buttered toast in a silver basket covered with an Irish linen napkin to keep it warm, strawberry preserves in a small ceramic jar with a tiny jam spoon, four-minute eggs hidden in handpainted eggcups, and a small vase of poseys in the center of the table looked almost like a still-life, back-lit by the morning sun.

Mr. Fell was examining a butterfly he had received in the mail. He held the butterfly up for Rosemary and Philip to inspect. Its wings were spread and affixed to a small pane of scientific glass. "A painted lady," he said. And then to Rosemary, as if it were a test: "Latin name . . ."

She answered instantly. "*Vanessa cardui*. They migrate, you know," she said to Philip. "Can you imagine that flying two thousand miles to a warmer climate? They look as though they could barely fight the wind."

Henry Fell put the butterfly down, carefully, so as not to bang the glass. "Very few of them survive the journey home the following year," he said. "But the females lay eggs along the way. And then the children do it again the following year."

Rosemary walked over to where her father was sitting. "Once, Papa, remember, when I was eight, we saw a flock . . ."

He corrected her, "A swarm . . ."

"A swarm of monarchs, like a patch of gold across the sky. We were in Connecticut . . ."

"And your mother was there. I remember," said Mr. Fell. He picked the butterfly up again and looked at it. "Is it instinct or sense that makes them do it?" he asked.

"Is there a difference?" asked Philip.

"Yes, I think there is," said Mr. Fell. "In more sensible times. You know we're sending more troops to France and Italy."

"What choice do we have?" said Philip.

"Don't you always have a choice about war?" asked Rosemary sounding female and pacifist and slightly petulant. "It's not as if we've been attacked. I sometimes think we may have entered into something that wasn't our business. I'm sorry. I have trouble making sense of it." She was quiet after this. She looked at Philip across the table. They had dressed in silence—neither of them mentioning the events the night before. It occurred to Rosemary, they should get their own place. Maybe, in their own apartment, there would be more room for honest interchange, less occasion to keep up appearances all of the time. She poured herself a cup of coffee and took a piece of buttered toast and topped it with preserves. Mr. Fell busied himself with the small note that had come with his butterfly. "Caught by the meadow at Sheepshead Bay, June 1, 1918."

"What are you doing today, dear?" Rosemary asked Philip, finally, after they had sat in a thick silence for a few minutes.

He looked surprised at the question. "I'm working," he said.

"You've been there every day since you got back. Don't you need a day off?"

Philip shook his head. "Teddy ran it by himself for

long enough. If you want to, you can meet me for lunch," he said.

"I have a lunch," said Rosemary, "one of those charity things. You'd just be bored . . . Then I'm working at the hospital." If she'd looked at his face, she might have had a different answer.

"Another time then," said Philip who shortly after that excused himself and went to work.

That day at lunch, he took a walk and, almost without meaning to, found himself on the street outside Miss Wetzel's Boarding House. There was a group of young boys playing stickball. Philip caught the ball as it almost rolled out into the street. He kicked it back. He considered taking off his jacket and joining them but they ran off. He stood across the street and looked up at Eleanor's window. The window was half-open, the curtain was blowing in the wind. And then he saw her framed in the window.

The street receded. There was darkness all around him and the piercing sound of an incoming shell as the night-sky exploded in a burst of light and next to him, the one they called "Dutch" because he was from Pennsylvania, no one knew his mother called him "Sweets", guts wrenched open spewing in the clay-red mud, writhed in agony and then lay motionless. Keep a cool facade. Can't let the men know you're afraid. Order the men to fire. No, don't. As, if they do, they'll only draw more fire on themselves. What was the rule, "Fire when fired on" . . . Was that the rule? Run. No. Retreat. A proper, provisional retreat, carried out before dawn. Make a list. Won't be able to take them with you, carry the dead on your back . . . or arrange a burial. Better, make a list so their families can be notified. Incoming . . . And the sky blasted white. Order the men to fire. No, don't. And Philip was left to wonder whether it was an act of cowardice—or self-preservation. He saw Eleanor framed in the window. And the words he'd written to her echoed in his mind, *"Did I speak to you about duty and honor . . . I meant to . . . Duty and honor. And what it's like to be bound to one thing when your heart wishes you to do something else,"* as the day crashed in on him again and he stared up at the empty window where she used to live.

He walked across the street and rang the bell although it was evident to him that she didn't live there anymore. Miss Wetzel opened the door and peered up at him. He hesitated. "I'm looking for Eleanor Smith," he said as politely and formally as he could. The bird-like woman shook her head. "Would you have an address?" She studied him for a moment—then left him in the open doorway as she reached in a drawer in the table for a slip of paper on which, in Eleanor's own hand, was written her address.

He took a taxi to her apartment building. As the cab pulled up and stopped at the curb, she walked out of the lobby on Robert Doyle's arm. Philip turned his head away so that she wouldn't see him, then looked back and watched as they walked down the street. She wasn't as thin as she had been, softer somehow yet moving with the same ease she'd always had, coltish, graceful. Her hair was straight, silken. Her skin unblemished. He watched her turn and look at Doyle and laugh at something that he'd said. Had he really expected she would wait for him?

He directed his taxi driver to take him to Jane Howard's address. And, once inside, demanded a whiskey.

"Have you even had lunch?" Jane asked him as she poured him a drink.

"When did you get so conservative?"

"I know," said Jane. "Isn't it peculiar?"

She handed him the scotch. He took a sip and sat down in an armchair. "Have you seen her?" he asked.

"Eleanor," said Jane. "Once." She chose these next words very carefully. "There was a period when she didn't go out much."

"Because of me?" he asked. He wondered if she'd heard about his death . . . or his return.

"That's best left between the two of you," said Jane.

"She's met someone else, hasn't she?"

Jane made a face. "You know when Rosemary was little," she said, "we used to play a game. I'd say 'blue' and she'd say . . . The grown-up version is, I'd say 'blue' and you'd say, 'Moon.' 'War' . . ."

Philip answered immediately, ". . . Crime."

Jane nodded. " 'Blue' . . . 'violet.' But whenever anyone else would play," she explained, "and they would say 'yellow' we would both say 'sun' or 'chicken', depending on our mood. But Rosemary and I always said the *same* thing usually at the same time."

She was trying to explain to him that she had switched sides, that it was one thing when they were playing in this, but now that it seemed real, her loyalty was to Rosemary.

"You haven't answered my question," said Philip.

"I'm glad you're back," she said. And then very formally added, "Can I get you another drink?"

Philip nodded, acknowledging the new rules between them.

eddy found him in the office a few hours later with a half-empty bottle of Jack Daniel's and a half-full glass. The mood at the docks was hushed, subdued.

An American carrier on its way to Britain had been hit the week before by German U-boats, less than a quarter of the crew had survived, and the ship had sunk, smashed and broken, in a mass of flames. It had been transporting civilian supplies, food, medicine, or as Teddy put it, "All this for potatoes and rubbing alcohol." And all ocean crossings had been delayed until passenger and cargo ships could be accompanied by military escort. Fleets of warships had been dispatched from England, France, and the United States. The seas were deserted except for the battalions and the German U-boats lurking under water just off the European shore.

Philip and Teddy had given their workers the week off but, not knowing what else to do with themselves, they showed up each morning, anyway, with bag lunches and dominoes and small children in tow and collected at the edge of the wharf idling away the afternoon, staring at the empty seas, as if their presence could somehow effect a speedier deployment.

Philip pulled another glass off the shelf for Teddy. "Join me," he said.

Teddy grabbed the glass that Philip had set out for him. "All right, I'll have one." He poured himself a drink. He sat down across from Philip at the desk. "We weren't better off without you, you know."

"Weren't you?" Philip asked him. "The business was fine. Rosemary lives in her own world. She's always fine. And if she's not, she rearranges the furniture." He took another sip of his drink. "You expect it's all going to wait for you," he said, "and it's all gone on without you." He hesitated. "Maybe it's me that's changed."

Outside the window, one of the men began to play

a mouth harp and the melody echoed, the waves breaking behind it almost like a bass-line. An ocean liner anchored out to sea, sat empty except for a three-man crew, as if it were a ghost hotel, swaying slightly on the flat, black waves and creaking on its moorings.

Jane convinced herself it was out of concern for Rosemary that she would finally tell her what she knew, true friendship, as it were, that Rosemary ought to know the facts, so that she could protect herself and do what she had to to hold on to Philip. Jane couldn't bear the thought that Philip had returned and Rosemary was at risk of losing him again.

She stopped and bought Rose flowers, a small arrangement of irises and bluebells that looked slightly patriotic. She found her in her bedroom, wearing a volunteer nurse's uniform, just sitting down to tea.

Jane held the bouquet out to her. "I brought you flowers."

Rosemary grabbed a small purple vase and disappeared for a moment to fill it with water. "They're beautiful," she said as she came out of the bathroom. "A little touch of spring." She set them on a table on the far side of the room, then sat down and poured herself a cup of tea.

"How are you?" asked Jane.

"Excellent," said Rosemary. "I feel like life has righted itself again."

"How's Philip?"

"Distant. God knows what he went through. They say it's normal. I don't care." She jumped up and began to slip off her uniform and button herself into a more stylish but comfortable dress. "He's home now and nothing else matters."

"I thought maybe we should have a party," she said. "Not big. A dinner party. Tomorrow night. Spontaneous." She sounded a little wistful. "The way we used to. Can you come?"

"Of course I can come," Jane answered. And then added, with a bit of an edge. "How are *you*, Jane? Did *you* have a nice day?" She hadn't meant to say it. It just slipped out. But Rosemary was so one-sided in the way she saw things, often missed what was going on around her, needed so badly to be shaken up.

Rosemary looked at her startled. "Have been I been self-obsessed lately, Jane. I'm sorry."

"No, I shouldn't have said that," said Jane. "I'm sorry. I have something to tell you, Rose."

"What?"

"Remember that—girl you picked up?"

"Yes, I remember," said Rosemary smiling. "Eleanor Smith. She sent me back the money that I gave her. As if it were a loan. Maybe I actually made a difference."

"I think *we* might have," said Jane.

"We?" said Rosemary. "What do you mean, 'we'?"

And then Jane confessed to her. "I followed her that night," she said. "I didn't feel right about sending her into the street. She was such a pretty girl. She looked as though no one had ever taken care of her."

Rosemary stared at Jane. It was hard to know which startled her more—that Jane had done something altruistic or that she'd kept it from her. Jane continued. "I gave her the address of Dora—Whitley, you know, my friend, the woman who owns the hat shop. I thought that she might work for her."

"Dora did the hats for my wedding," Rosemary said in crisp staccato tones, as if she were insisting that it wasn't true. "I never saw her there."

"Philip did."

Rosemary cut her off. "I don't want to hear this."

"But you must. You have to hear this."

"No, I don't have to hear this, Jane. I don't want to hear it. It was all so long ago, wasn't it? Over a year. I mean, since the wedding. It has been the longest year. It's not still going on, is it—whatever was going on? I don't—want to hear this. You've always been jealous of me." And then she turned on Jane with surprising force. "I was all the dreams you never had," she said. She was almost screaming. "You've never really wanted my life to be all right. You've never had your own life, Jane. All you've ever done is meddle in other people's lives."

"That's not true. I've had a life. You've never chosen to be part of it. You only let me in to your part."

"Do I owe you an apology, Jane? Perhaps I do. But I don't want to hear this other part."

"No, I'm sure you don't," said Jane. "She has a child. I'm sorry," she said, as if an apology could make any of this fine again. "I thought you should know."

In that moment, Rosemary seemed nearly implacable. She retreated, into her manners and breeding, and became so remote and distant and formal that it was impossible for Jane to do anything except excuse herself and leave the room.

"I've had the oddest talk with Jane," said Rosemary that night when Philip was lying in bed. She was sitting at the vanity with her back to him but she could see him in the mirror. He didn't answer her.

"In a way, she's the most alone person I know," said Rosemary as she continued to brush her hair.

"Is she, Rose?" asked Philip.

"Well, she doesn't have anyone except her mother and who knows how long that will last." She got up and sat beside Philip on the bed. "If something happened to Papa," she said, "I don't know what I'd do." She looked at him waiting for some response. "Of course, I have my own family now." She put a hand lightly on his forehead. "If something were to happen to you . . ."

"You?" said Philip. "You'd be fine."

"Would I, Philip? You just think I'd be fine." Did she want him to reassure her? Did she want him to tell her that he'd never leave her . . . She leaned in and kissed him as if in that moment she could shut out the world.

$\mathcal{E}$leanor was sitting on the grass in Central Park, a Victorian picture of sorts, her long skirt spread about her, all her attention focussed on Tess, who was lying on a blanket, playing with an ivory and silver teething toy in the shape of a bell.

"Yes," said Eleanor, "that's good grabbing." She reached her hand in and helped Tess shake the bell. "See, if you shake it like this," she said, "it makes a sound."

The baby's face broke into a smile as Eleanor reached in and turned her over on her back and began to tickle her. The noonday sun felt warm on her back.

And then she was aware of a shadow on the grass, a woman's form.

Rosemary had shown up first thing that morning at Jane Howard's door. Jane was still in her dressing gown having stayed up much too late the night before drinking wine. She offered Rose coffee, which she refused. "No, I won't come in," she said. "You're giving me Eleanor Smith's address." And Jane complied, writing it on a piece of note-paper from a tawdry mid-town hotel where she had recently spent an afternoon with a young woman she had met at the make-up counter at Best & Co.

"I can't tell you to be gentle with her," said Jane as she handed her the address, "because I don't think that's what she deserves."

Secretly, she was pleased because she'd expected Rose to fight for this.

Eleanor wasn't at the apartment. Rosemary was told by Josie Kennedy who answered the door that she had gone to the park. The park. Of course. That's where you went with a baby. Philip's baby lying on the quilt.

And then she was aware of a shadow on the grass, a woman's form.

She looked up and saw Rosemary looking down at her.

"Did I do something to you?" asked Rosemary. "I'm trying to understand this. I brought you home for tea. I gave you money. It was an act of kindness. I thought—it was an act of kindness."

Eleanor was too startled to answer her.

And then as suddenly as she was there, she was gone, and the shadow on the grass had become sunlight again. Eleanor sat there for a moment alone on the quilt with her baby.

When she got back to the lobby of her building, there was a man standing, leaning against one of the marble pillars. She recognized him at once. She braced herself and pushed the baby's carriage toward the elevator.

"What is it," she asked as she passed him, "family day? I just saw your wife." Philip barely reacted as he was trying to register what he hadn't known before, that he had a child.

"Is it?" he asked looking at Tess.

"Your baby?" she said immediately. "I don't know. With girls like me you never can be sure. Of course, it's your baby." She was almost crying.

Philip stepped into her. He started to kiss her face and smooth away her tears with the palm of his hand.

"I didn't know," he said. "Believe me when I tell you that I didn't know." He realized he respected her more because she'd never told him, that she would never ask him for anything, that any decision he would make would have to be his own.

He lifted her hair softly and kissed her on the nape of the neck. "Believe me," he said again, softly, "when I tell you that I didn't know. Shh. I'm here now." He kissed her on the cheek and then the mouth. "And I'm not going to leave you."

Before he left, he promised her that he would come back to her that night. He could no longer live with Rosemary . . . but he had to tell her. Had to make her understand that she would be better off without him, better off with someone who was much more like her kind. In time, he reasoned, she would forgive him. She would find someone else. But how was he to tell her. . . .

He reached in and picked up the baby, his baby, from the carriage and held her to him and then leaned in and kissed Eleanor again.

*I*t was dark when he came home. The steps to the house looked steep, ominous, as though there were more of them than there had been before. There was no easy way to do this, no good time to do this. He stood on the street for a long time considering how he would tell her. And then let himself into the house.

He practically walked into Gertrude who was carrying a silver tray of hors d'oeuvres into the living room. "Damn!" He'd forgotten they were having a dinner party. He went to the living room and poured himself a drink. Charlie Miles, the piano player from the club, had been hired for the evening and was sitting on the bench at the piano. He was dressed in a tuxedo with a ruffled shirt and a 2-cent carnation in his lapel and his arms fairly hung below the seat of the piano bench as he sat there as relaxed as if he were a rag doll.

Charlie Miles started to play a melody with a bass-line that was early speakeasy, haunting, Victorian, but with a hint of blues to come.

∽

Rosemary was upstairs dressing; that is, she had spread four dresses out on the bed and was trying to figure out which one to wear, as if she could reinvent herself and it would all be fine.

She sat down at the vanity. She started to put kohl under her eyes but she was too nervous to sit. She walked back to the bed and picked up a pale blue taffeta dress that was off the shoulder. She was holding it up to herself in the mirror when Philip walked into the room.

"Hi, I was—getting worried about you," she said. "You're so late. You need to change. You'll be late for dinner. The Portervilles are coming and the Fergusons . . ."

"Rosemary," said Philip trying in vain to stop her going on.

"They have a new baby," she said. "A boy. I told

them not to bring him. I can't stand it when everyone stands around goo goo over a new baby. It just stops a dinner party cold. And Jane's coming, I think."

Philip just stood there looking at her. "Rose, I have something to tell you . . ." he said.

"Which dress do you like better, dear?" she asked him holding up a beige silk gown that was cut on the bias.

"Rose, stop!" he said more forcefully than he meant to. "Shall we discuss where to put the chair or which necklace you should wear? Or better yet where I should sit? Or where you should place me like that porcelain box over there."

She put the dress down. "I don't think of you as a fixture, Philip," she said. "Sit down, dear," and then she stopped realizing she'd just directed him again. "I'm sorry."

He stood there looking at her. "I think you are the one who ought to sit down, Rose," he said finally. They both continued to stand.

She knew what he was going to tell her.

"I can't—I can't live here anymore, Rose," he said.

"What do you think of New Orleans?" she asked immediately. "I hear it's a nice—" But she realized this wasn't going to play, it wasn't the city he was referring to. "It isn't true, Philip." She turned on him. She knew she sounded hysterical. "It isn't true,

Philip." She took a deep breath. "We—we ought to have gone away when you got back. We needed some time away. We never had a honeymoon." She knew she sounded desperate but it didn't matter to her.

"Don't do this, Rose," he said. "It isn't you. Since I've been back I've—your life is perfect, Rose. It's me that doesn't fit into it."

"Did I do something . . . ?" she asked almost as if she hadn't heard anything he'd said to her. "I—can change. I can be anything you want me to be. It—isn't true, Philip."

"Since I've been back, I've tried," he said. "Maybe I haven't tried as hard as I should have . . ."

He reached out to touch her hair and somehow the softness of the act infuriated her, as though it were evidence to her that he did love her. "It isn't true," she said again.

But he went on. "But your life—our life would never have made either of us happy."

She walked away from him. She walked over to the vanity and looked at herself in the mirror. Her voice got deeper. "I know I can be cold," she said. "Sometimes I'm so involved in—I'll be better, Philip."

"It isn't any use, Rose," he said. "There isn't anything you can do. I've fallen in love with someone else."

"You just think you have," she said and the sound of her own voice frightened her. She hardly heard the next few things he said to her.

"I know it isn't fair . . ."

"I know you think I can take care of myself," she interrupted him.

"I know I made a vow to you," he said.

She spoke on top of him. "I know you think I don't need anything. But it isn't true. When I thought you were—" She was hysterical now, "but I knew you were never. I knew you were coming back to me." And then she was almost screaming. "What makes you think that she can make you happy? She can't make you happy. Because she needs you to take care of her?"

She'd gone too far for Philip. He turned to go.

And she went after him. "What makes her think that she can have what's mine!" Her left hand closed over the handle of the letter opener on the vanity. "She can't have what's mine."

She touched him on the shoulder and when he turned, in one swift motion, in a mixture of rage and anger so precise that her aim and movement were unavoidable as he raised his arm to defend himself a moment too late, she stabbed him in the throat.

He gasped as his hand went to his throat and then fell to the floor.

From downstairs, she heard the sound of the front door closing as the first of the guests arrived. And the beginning strains of piano music from the party below.

The piano music was sedate, a little bit romantic. None of the guests thought that it was odd that neither Philip or Rosemary had come down, they were often late for their own engagements. Teddy was in a fabulous mood. He had a new suit on and he couldn't keep his feet from dancing. He turned to his wife, Sarah, and said, "I can't believe you don't know the Castle Walk." He gestured to the piano player to start it up and set his champagne glass on the mantel and demonstrated a few steps, then took Sarah by the waist and started to "walk" her about the room. Always game, she picked it up at once. Everyone was laughing. The music got a little louder. And then Rosemary opened the door to the parlor. Teddy and Sarah stopped dancing almost as if they were frozen in their spot. There was blood on Rosemary's dress and where her hand touched the wall, was a stain of blood, as well. She stood there framed in the doorway. "Mr. Alsop," she said, "Philip, will not be joining us for dinner."

It was Jane who went upstairs and found his body lying on the floor.

Teddy had the presence of mind to telephone the authorities. The police came. There was an ambulance outside. They carried Philip down the stairs on a stretcher his face and body covered with a sheet. The police car or the ambulance car's light was flashing making circles of red in the entranceway.

And then they took Rosemary away, as well. Jane insisted that they let her change her dress. She'd put her hair up. Her hands were handcuffed behind her back. There was a policeman on either side of her. She didn't say a word, just went along with them as though she were an actor acting out a final scene.

Eleanor gave Tess a bath and put her in a velvet dress. She spent a long time brushing her own hair, put on a dress she'd never worn before, gray silk, a little low in front with lots of buttons. She made a simple dinner and set the table with what good china they had and lit two ivory tapers.

Josie had agreed to spend the night at a friend's. She poured herself a glass of white wine and told Tess a lot of silly things about the way she thought their life would be. And when it got late, she thought a number of other things, that she was a fool for believing him. Of course, he'd never leave for her. That he just hadn't known how to tell Rosemary and to-morrow it would all be fine. *It would be fine, wouldn't it?* In the distance, she heard the sound of a siren. She couldn't bring herself to eat.

She put Tess in a nightgown and put her in her crib. She was cold. She looked at the clock. It was after ten. She took the silk shawl Philip had bought for her from a drawer and wrapped it around her shoulders. Outside, she heard a carriage. She ran to the window but it continued on. She shut the curtains to the room. She walked back to the baby's crib and sang to her—

Hush little baby, don't say a word.
Papa's gonna buy you a mockingbird.
And if that mockingbird don't sing,
Papa's gonna buy you a diamond ring . . .

She realized that he wasn't coming. It was only when she saw the papers two days later that she knew the reason why.

BOOKS BY AMY EPHRON

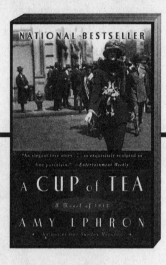

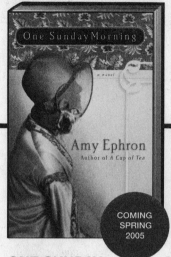

COMING
SPRING
2005

A CUP OF TEA
A Novel of 1917

ISBN 0-06-078620-5 (paperback)

A Cup of Tea is a tale of romance set against the backdrop of New York society during the uncertain days of World War I. It is brought to life by its vivid (and often amusing) cast of characters, its wonderful period detail of New York's drawing rooms and hat shops, and by its delightfully spare and picturesque sense of story.

ONE SUNDAY MORNING
A Novel

ISBN 0-06-058552-8 (hardcover)

A story set in 1920s New York, in which four women at a bridge party see another woman, whom they all know, come out of a hotel with a man who isn't her husband. The four women make a pact not to tell anyone, but it's only a matter of time before one of them does and the truth is far from what it seems.